Drugs War

Following the paths of honest men is not easy for either Ahmed or Hamid. Their choices have an impact far beyond the boundaries of their villages. Thousands of miles away, in foreign lands, strangers are making decisions, too…

To the rest of the world – the deadly and illegal trade of hallucinogenic drugs is an anathema, abhorrent, to be fought without fear or favour… but in Afghanistan where villagers have no other source of income… what else can they do?

William Taylor

Born in 1920 and educated at Godalming County School in Surrey, after an electrical engineering apprenticeship, William Taylor joined the Royal Air Force just after the start of the Second World War. Injuries in 1946 ended his RAF career, so he then pursued a career in electronics and computers.

He is registered blind and is a member of St. Dunstans, the Association for blind ex Service men and Women. Notwithstanding his sight problem he continues to use all aspects of computing. In conjunction with a friend he has published several books on Management and Finance. He is able to write using special programs. William is married to Eileen and has one daughter and two sons.

Watch www.uppublications.ltd.uk for more information

First published in Great Britain in 2011 by U P Publications Ltd

Head Office: 25 Bedford Street, Peterborough, UK. PE1 4DN

A CIP Catalogue record of this book is available from the British Library

ISBN 978-1-908135-05-6

Printed in England by The Lightning Source Group

FIRST EDITION

www.uppublications.ltd.uk

Drugs War

William Taylor

U P Publications
2011

To my patient wife Eileen,
with thanks for the encouragement and support
given by all my family.

1

In the rocky terrain of a village in the hills of Afghanistan a heavily bearded man watched the narrow winding path leading upwards from the deep valley below. He sat on a large flat rock with a rough shelter over his head made of branches and leaves to protect him from the fierce sun. It was a boring job and the men of the village took turns to watch during the daylight hours.

At night, a barrier was placed across the path with bells on it to warn of any movement. This precaution had never been tested so whether it would have given the villagers enough time to escape from any danger is doubtful but they felt better for its presence.

The job, however boring, was judged to be very important, as two enemies might come up from the valley floor. One was remnants of the Taliban who would steal the village crops and anything else they could find; the women also would be at risk. The Taliban had been soundly thrashed in the war between them and the Nato Alliance. It had been a bloody affair and the Afghan forces had contributed nobly but with enormous losses.

After the Alliance had withdrawn from a fighting role the Afghan army was rebuilt with the help of British and American trainers. It took several years for this to be achieved but the policy was clear; the Taliban must not come back.

The other enemy was the Afghan police or army who would destroy the crops and probably burn the whole village but they were not too active at the moment so the villagers believed they might be safe from them for the time being.

The village was situated on a small fertile plain nestling in the hills and with the mountains in the distance surrounding the area. There were a large number of paths from the village spreading out into the hills and mountains beyond. The villagers knew these paths well, but strangers would have found it very difficult to find their way. The paths had been formed over centuries and were a network over the whole area.

The villagers used the path down to the valley very occasionally for their main transport needs as the path eventually turned into a lane and then into a road. The road split into many ways again making it difficult to find the village.

For secret journeys, they always used the paths through the hills. This isolation was perfect for growing the opium poppy, *papaver somniferum,* the sale of the opium providing a fair living for the villagers. The poppies were grown in a large field at one side of the village together with maize; the latter helped to minimise the weeds as well as providing feed for animals.

The position of the field was perfect for growing the opium poppy plant as it was sun-drenched for many hours of the day. It was also many metres above sea level, which suited the crop. The poppy pods were cut carefully in the late afternoon the previous day; the opium latex had then run out overnight and coagulated ready for collection. When it was scraped off into jars, it was taken to the large open-fronted shed, which stood at the side of the field. Several of the able-bodied men and women were working on the latex that had been removed from the poppy pods.

When all the latex had been collected the pods were removed from the plant and dried in the sun; the seeds inside would be used for the next crop and the opium sold after some purification. On this very hot morning, the villagers were busy working at their various tasks; the environment was peaceful and quiet. All the activity was to provide the villagers a share in the proceeds of the sale of the opium.

Suddenly, there was a loud blast from a single-toned horn blown by one of the villagers, who also pointed to the sky. He had heard the distant sound of an aeroplane or helicopter.

The reaction was immediate throughout the small village.

Abdullah, the head man, shouted for everyone to hide but the people were already moving fast. It was a well-practised manoeuvre; raffia screens were dropped hastily over the front of the opium and donkey sheds.

In less than a minute the village looked dead; the remnants of the maize in the field helping the illusion. The man looking out to the valley floor crouched back under his layer of branches to avoid any detection. The heavy drone of a helicopter came nearer and soon it circled overhead. The police inspector aboard turned to the pilot and said, "It looks abandoned but let's have a closer look." The pilot nodded and moved nearer the ground.

"Cannot see any movement or sign of life sir."

"Nor can I, but let's go round again and a bit lower if you can," replied the policeman and the pilot circled the village again, even lower than before.

"Nothing there I think sir."

"I agree, it looks empty, let's go home," replied the policeman.

Abdullah had been watching from his camouflaged hideaway and as soon as the helicopter noise could no longer be heard he shouted, "All clear, you can come out now," and on this instruction the man with the horn blew two quick blasts. Such action had occurred before and the village was used to occasional visits in the sky. What they did not want was a visit from the valley as they had no protection from a land-based assault. All they could do if someone came was to grab their possessions, including their opium, and disappear into the hills where they would be safe as no one could find them, but the village might not be there when they returned. Abdullah was worried that one day some eagle-eyed policeman would notice a sign that would give away their careful camouflaging. He was more correct than he supposed, as time would reveal.

Abdullah was born in this village and had always been well thought of so he naturally graduated into the headman position. He was about one hundred and eighty centimetres tall, and had a large moustache on a handsome and kind face. He was well known for his honesty and care for others: an ideal candidate for his position. He often wondered about his cousin, Hamid Rahim, in Meyhabul, a town some way away from the village. He used to see Hamid in the local town of Ghazi rat when they were children. Hamid went away early in their lives so they had never met since. He thought that Hamid surely had a good job that did not require him to hide as they did. In fact, Hamid did not have to hide but his job was anything but good.

That day, after the helicopter went away, work continued in the village; they planned to sell some opium to buy provisions. The village was a community where they all shared in the provisions purchased by the opium sale. The seedpods had discharged their evil load and the next job was to purify the opium. At present, there were odd bits of leaves and other organic matter mixed in with the opium; this must be removed.

A select few of the villagers, supervised by Abdullah, were converting the basic opium into a more valuable version. They dissolved the opium in large, battered, cooking pots of boiling water, which left twigs, leaves and other organic rubbish unaffected. They then strained the opium solution through muslin cloths and dried the resulting liquid in the sun to evaporate the water.

Abdullah examined the final putty-like product and pronounced he was satisfied. Now he must send the opium to the town of Ghazi rat some twenty kilometres from the village. A few days later, three heavily loaded donkeys set off along one of the many paths leading out of the village through the hills. The journey would take at least two days, as travel was slow in the rough terrain and great care had to be taken to avoid detection.

The delivered opium would be passed on to a larger concern where it would, in all probability, be turned into heroin. It was a chemical process, which the villagers were happy for someone else to carry out; they were content merely to sell the refined opium. Some of the larger opium growers carried out the whole process but Abdullah and the elders of the village had opted for the village to be just a grower and collector of the opium.

The men set off on their hard journey; the paths were narrow and the surfaces hard to walk on, as they were so uneven. The donkeys, laden as they were, seemed not to notice the rough paths, treading delicately but firmly on their way. The men found the going much more difficult. They plodded on until dusk, when they stopped to eat a simple meal and sleep just off the trail until early morning. When they awoke, they had a little food and plodded on until late afternoon of the second day.

The dangerous time for the two men and their valuable load was about a quarter of a kilometre from the town when the police might come across the delivery. They grew more tense as they neared their destination. The feet of the donkeys were wrapped in cloths to ensure a quieter approach and the two men listened for any noise indicating danger. The worst part was where they had to cross about one hundred and fifty metres of open ground towards the building where they hoped for a good price for their cargo.

They waited until dusk and then hurried over the final distance to the building. All seemed well and they knocked on the door as quietly as possible. A small shutter opened in the door and a voice said, "What do you want?"

"We come from the village."

"There are many villages," came the ironic reply.

"We are from Abdullah's village," the men said.

"Why did you not say so in the first place," came the reply, "come in, and quickly!" The small shutter in the door closed and the large door opened. The two men and their donkeys went inside the open quadrangle and the large door closed quickly behind them.

After unloading the opium their contact at the premises carefully examined and weighed the opium. He told them the price he would pay and, as usual, the number of Afghanis quoted was really a take it or leave it price. They tried to negotiate for a little more but the buyer was implacable. The villagers finally agreed but were not happy about it; lately the buying price seemed to get lower each time.

After business was completed they had a meal with some wine and a short rest. Their next job was to buy provisions to take back to the village. Abdullah had provided them with a large list of goods required and it should again load the three donkeys to capacity. Unfortunately, as they found out, the money they had received for the opium was not quite enough to obtain all the items on Abdullah's list. They had to buy a little less of some items. The premises they were in, was ostensibly a general store selling all things from food to ironmongery but the most profitable part was said to be the movement of opium and other drugs.

The two men fed their donkeys and they all retired to a small shed where they slept until early morning. After loading the donkeys with the provisions and carefully checking the money secreted on their persons they set off on the return journey. They were as careful in leaving as they were in arriving, as they had no wish to make the acquaintance with authority or robbers. In one sense, this return journey was not as dangerous, as they were not carrying the opium. If the authorities did happen to catch up with them, they were not doing anything illegal. On the other hand, they had provisions, drink and the opium money, so there was danger from robbers.

They were also in constant danger of the police or other government agent becoming suspicious, although tracking their route back would not have been an easy task. They were very careful and often stopped to look and listen for anyone following them. They were as lucky again on this expedition as they had been on many previous ones and returned to Abdullah with the money and provisions. The entire village was pleased to see the men back and, as always, a simple celebration was held that night.

In the morning, Abdullah spoke to the men about the money. He had noticed that the price for the same amount of opium had been gradually getting smaller. He trusted the men implicitly, that was not the problem. The men said they thought the same but did not know what to do about it. If they started to bargain, they were simply told to try elsewhere. Abdullah nodded, he must think about this, as the money was not enough to sustain the village life as it used to be.

He did give some thought to other possible activities the village might carry out to earn money but could not think of any. After dwelling on his problem overnight, he decided he must go to Ghazi rat and see what he could do about the opium price. Putting his second in command in charge of the village, he took a companion with him. When they reached the town, they went into the business, which dealt with the opium. Abdullah was well known and received courteously.

After some time the subject of the opium price was discussed and a few hours later Abdullah was able to get a promise that the price would be improved. Abdullah returned home pleased that he had been able to achieve a result but was still concerned whether the increase was enough. He continued to think about this as he walked. He did not notice the police detective who tracked him for a large part of his journey.

Four days later a messenger arrived from the business in Ghazi rat to tell Abdullah that they believed his journey route had been compromised; Police were talking about a raid at some future date. This had never occurred before and Abdullah cursed at his own carelessness. He moved quickly to put matters right as best as he could. Villagers were dispatched to the farthest intersection and large rocks were placed to block the original trail. Earth was bonded into the rocks and plants placed so as to look natural. The same thing was done at a nearer interchange and the two would confuse a possible intruder or perhaps give some warning.

It took five days of intensely hard toil to get this work done as the rocks were very heavy and had to be moved from other places. The appearance had to be natural, which was a difficult task. Abdullah told the villagers how grateful he was for their efforts and apologised again for his carelessness. He knew that unless the correct paths were followed a person could wander the hills for days and still not find the village.

Unknown to Abdullah another problem was arising that could have future ramifications. The police officer who had viewed the village from the helicopter went back after the flight to enter his report in the daybook. He wrote, "No sign of life, considered to be an empty village." As he turned to go home, his shift having finished, a fleeting thought entered his mind but was quickly lost. He shook his head, puzzled as to what it was but soon decided that it was imagination and quickly forgot the incident.

Several months later, when he was off duty and relaxing with his wife and children, the thought came again, and this time it stuck. What had he seen in the village? He strained to think and then knew what was odd about that helicopter visit. He had seen what appeared to be impossible, a rock that moved. He decided to pay another visit when the helicopter was free.

After the warning from the business, Abdullah was anxious but two months passed and no intruders appeared... He grew even more relaxed as the time passed and nothing untoward happened.

Events however were taking place many hundreds of kilometres away, which could impinge upon this simple village life and many other small and large opium growers.

2

Abdullah's cousin, Hamid Rahim, did not have the pleasant job that Abdullah had imagined. He sweated profusely as he loaded the never-ending supply of boxes from the loading bay into the waiting lorries. This was the main wholesale fruit and vegetable market in Meyhabul, a large town one hundred and fifty kilometres from Ghazi rat where Abdullah sold his opium.

Hamid had worked in this market for ten long and weary years. He was a man of medium height, well built with powerful shoulders and arms. He was good looking in a rough sort of way with strong features and jet black hair. Due to the constant bending at his work he was unable to straighten his back completely. It was only a slight fault in what was a good shaped body.

He tried to straighten now as he hitched up his linen trousers, took off his hat and wiped the sweat from his forehead. He rested for a moment and thought – if only he had a decent wage for all this hard work. His mind had been in turmoil for several years with his inability to earn more money.

He thought of his Uncle and his wealth, which most people believed was obtained from the illegal drugs trade. Hamid had only visited his Uncle once much earlier in his life and he remembered the great house with its grounds and horses.

"Rahim," came the unpleasant voice of the supervisor,

"You get paid to work not to daydream." The voice of the supervisor cracked across the concrete and Hamid gave an involuntary jump. He turned to look at the owner of the voice, a short man with a large stomach, long greasy hair and a large nose: an ugly individual. Hamid hated him, it was unjust, just a short rest that was all. If only he could do something like his Uncle and leave this hot and sweaty job for good.

"Well?" the supervisor shouted.

Hamid hurriedly started loading the boxes again. He felt that the supervisor was always watching him and he wished something terrible would happen to him. The anger that he felt was boiling over. Since this new supervisor had come, some six months ago, life had become very unbearable. He must get out of this job and the figures kept coming into his head. Just a few thousand Afghanis; perhaps, that was all he needed to make a start and enter the drugs trade. He had one advantage he thought, he was sure his Uncle would provide some know how. A few thousand Afghanis; then he thought again, it might as well be nothing, it would never be enough.

At lasts his work for that day cane to an end.

Hamid decided he could not go back to this soul-destroying job whatever the consequences. Then he thought again – what could he do? He and his wife had to live, and a poor life it was in any case. Then he thought about the moneylender. He knew of other people who said they were going to borrow some money; did they succeed Hamid asked himself?

He decided he would try, after he had been back to his home and had a meal; his mind might be clearer after that. The moneylender seemed always to be available but Hamid knew deep down that his chances of getting a loan were not high. Still he must try; he could not work at the market any longer. He had come to the end of his tether. Unfortunately, he gave no real thought as to how he could pay back a loan. He arrived home to find his wife in a bad mood.

"What ails you wife?" Hamid asked her. He was nonplussed, never having seen his wife crying like this before. He could not tell her now about his plans and that he did not intend to return to his work tomorrow. His wife looked up and said,

"I'm fed up with this life. We are always scraping a bare living, you bring home a pittance and sometimes hardly any food; I would like it to change." She continued, "We never go out anywhere, we do nothing."

Hamid had never heard his wife complain before and was taken aback with both the statement and the vehement way she had said it. His initial reaction was to feel guilty, he knew he had not provided much comfort for his wife but jobs were very difficult. He wondered whether this was the right time to tell her of all his plans to leave work and try to get some money to start a drugs business.

He decided it would be right to tell her about trying to do something else but not about leaving his job now so he said, "I've decided to do something about it as I'm just as fed up as you are, especially since this new overseer has been in charge. This man is ruining my life and I must change it in some way."

"What can you do?" asked his wife.

"I'm going to ask my Uncle to help me"

His wife laughed ironically, "He's refused before. True it was a long time ago, but what makes you think he will be any different this time?"

"It has got to be," replied Hamid, "I'm going to make sure this time." His wife shrugged her shoulders and said no more. She had no faith that her husband could get out of this trap. He had no particular skills. She loved him but knew what he could and could not do. He also pondered whether to see the moneylender first or get in touch with his Uncle before doing so. Eventually he decided to try to get some money first; his Uncle might then feel more inclined to help. Hamid sat down to eat the simple meal that his wife had prepared: all their meals were simple. They could not afford much. Afterwards, Hamid set off to the moneylender: he knew his chances were slim.

The moneylender lived in a large house in a quiet road about two kilometres away. It had a large square lawn in front and borders of flowers around. Most of the houses in this street were of a superior nature and Hamid wondered how they all made enough money to have such places. He was to discover more about this in the months to come. He walked up the drive to the moneylender's house, getting more nervous with each step of the way. He knocked on the large wooden door and his heart was racing. Why would the moneylender bother with such a person as himself let alone give him any money? He nearly turned and ran back down the drive but suddenly the door opened and an attractive lady appeared.

She asked, "Can we help you?" Hamid was stuck for an answer for a moment then said, "I would like to see the..." he faltered and was unable to finish the sentence.

"The moneylender?" the lady queried.

"Yes, yes, that's right," stuttered Hamid.

"Come in then," the lady replied with a quiet smile at Hamid, "He will not be long." Hamid's nerves were even more on edge than before and again he wanted to run away.

At that moment the moneylender entered the room and Hamid was trying to think what to say. Could he persuade the moneylender to help him? The moneylender said,

"My name is Hedayat Khasi, do sit down." He seemed a pleasant man, tall and good-looking and dressed immaculately in an expensive suit. He was much younger than Hamid had imagined. "So, what can I do for you?" he asked.

Hamid wriggled uncomfortably in his seat, and managed a croaky, "I want to borrow some money."

"Well, that's what I thought you might be here for, how much?" The moneylender sat back in his chair waiting for Hamid to speak. Hamid was feeling distinctly unsure of himself and realised now he had not thought the process through at all.

"Well, I, I," he stammered.

"Perhaps I can help," said the moneylender. Hamid nodded, his mind was in a whirl, and he had no idea at all what he wanted. He waited for the moneylender to continue. "Perhaps you could tell me what you want the money for?"

Hamid had no real answer to give and only a weak, "I want to do something else."

The moneylender gave a wry smile; here was a very confused individual. Should he waste any more time with him or should he tell him to go. He decided to try for a while longer as a thought was formulating in his mind. He considered for a moment and then said,

"Tell me more about the job you are in and why you want to move."

Hamid felt easier about this question and was soon telling his story – how he worked so hard for so little and all about the new supervisor. The moneylender listened patiently until Hamid had finished. "What would you really like to do?" he enquired.

"I'd like to get into the same business as my Uncle, he deals in various, er, chemicals."

The moneylender smiled and after a moment said, "You mean illegal drugs?" Hamid's face flushed and he made no comment. The moneylender continued, "I thought that might be the reason; you see I know your Uncle very well. I have had dealings with him in the past." Hamid smiled guiltily and wriggled again in his seat. "I would strongly advise you to have as little contact with your Uncle as you can. He moves in some seriously dangerous circles and certainly not those in which you would want to be involved."

What good advice this was, would be proved in the months to come. There was a pause while Hamid tried to absorb what he had been told. The moneylender spoke again, "I have a suggestion; you can work for me and we will sort out your problems over time. I want some debts collected and my previous man has recently left me." Hamid was delighted with this offer and stammered his thanks.

"Tomorrow we will give you a list of debtors who want chasing. I want a hard approach but no violence and if any is used against you, just retire from it and let me deal with it. So far, I have had no police interference and naturally, I want to keep it that way. Apart from the one or two that might come into this category I do want results," he added in a brisker tone of voice. "Now go and see my secretary about your wages and duties."

Hamid again thanked the moneylender profusely and walked into the Secretary's office. He realised at that moment that this job would require his full attention; he would be free at last from the terrible job at the wholesale warehouse. After some time with the secretary learning more details about what he would have to do he was told the amount of wages he would receive.

Hamid was too excited to say much after hearing the number of Afghanis per week he would receive and, after all the formalities were complete, rushed home to tell his wife the good news. His wife could hardly believe what she was told and the two of them relaxed over a cup of tea to celebrate their good fortune. While they were enjoying this, his wife was thinking to herself that this job would stop her husband's ambitions to contact his Uncle. If she could have seen the future, she would not have been so happy.

The next day Hamid reported to the house of the moneylender and went into the office of the secretary. The lady was already there and said, "Good morning Hamid, I have the list of collections for you." Hamid took the list and replied,

"Thank you, I will get started right away."

The secretary smiled and said, "Good luck," and Hamid set off to his first call. He noticed that the secretary had arranged his calls so that he would not have to double back on his travels.

The first few people he visited were no problem; they came to the door straight away and paid all that was required. Hamid thought this was an easy job; he felt he would enjoy it, as it was pleasant walking around the various parts of the town.

On approaching the next house on his round, it was evident that this was ostensibly a house of some distinction. Hamid wondered why there should be debt here. He knocked on the door but there was no answer. He knocked again but still no one came and Hamid walked to the back of the house. He saw a woman hanging out some washing so he called to her at the back entrance and told her his business.

"Oh, he'll have to wait, I can't pay this week."

Hamid pointed out politely that this would only make the debt worst. He said, "Why not pay something otherwise I don't know want the moneylender might do." The woman thought about this veiled threat and said,

"All right I will have to pay I suppose."

Hamid took the money, marked her off in his book and resumed his travels. He knocked at the next place and a voice said, "Who are you and what do you want?"

"I come from the moneylender," replied Hamid.

"You will have to wait a minute," the voice came from inside. Eventually the door opened and Hamid was more than surprised to find that the local mayor's wife stood in the doorway. He had seen the Mayor and his wife at a public meeting a few months ago so he recognised her. After consulting his book, he told the mayor's wife the amount she should pay. Afterwards Hamid thought to himself that he was not the only one who was occasionally short of money, but he was greatly surprised to see others on his round who he would never have thought were in debt. At least he did not owe anything himself, even though he was much poorer than the people on these streets were. According to the houses they lived in, they should be much better off. Hamid continued with his rounds and found the walking a healthy pursuit. He had virtually forgotten all about his Uncle and his own previous ambitions.

It was several months later that on one of his regular visits to the Mayor's house the Mayor himself answered the door. He looked closely at Hamid and said, "I believe your surname is Rahim, is that right?"

"Yes, my name is Hamid Rahim."

The Mayor said, "Then I have a letter from your Uncle, Omar Rahim. He sent it to me because he did not have your address. I will get it for you." The Mayor returned a minute later and handed the letter to Hamid, who thanked him. Hamid was intrigued at the receipt of this message from his Uncle. Why would his Uncle write to him after such a long time? He put the letter safely away in his pocket until he arrived home.

As soon as his work was finished he hurried back to see his wife. He said, "What do you think happened today?"

She replied, "I have no idea, what did happen?"

Hamid told her about the letter; she was not happy about it as she thought it might change their life again. She waited with some apprehension as Hamid opened the letter; she could not know how right her prediction was, about changes to come.

Hamid was surprised at the contents of the letter and the fact that he had received one at all from his uncle. He could not know that, in less than a year, its contents would influence fate's decision, on whether he should live or die.

3

Pedro Sanchez waited in the large wood panelled hall in the comfortable chair indicated for him by a secretary. He was in the Ministry of Foreign Affairs of the Spanish Government in Madrid.

A week before he had been asked by a junior minister to be available to attend the Ministry within a few hours, when called. He had not been told the reason. He was of course extremely curious about the message and could not think why he had any business with Foreign Affairs. He might have business with the Ministry of the Interior but attendance at Foreign Affairs was strange. Idly, he scanned the few magazines piled neatly near the visitors' chairs. Concentration on any particular item was difficult – he wanted to get this appointment over. Sanchez was not used to the inactivity of waiting in offices and fidgeted in the chair.

He was a handsome man, very fit, and thirty-five years old. He ran regularly eight kilometres through the 'El Parque de Retiro', and the 'Calle de Alfonso' on his way to Police headquarters. He had tenseness about him, like a coiled spring, a busy man who sought continuous results. He was in control of some three hundred and fifty detectives and other staff and operated one of the most successful police units in Spain if not in Europe. Crime had reduced to low levels since he had been in charge some three years ago. The main problem he faced in his work was the increasing pressure from the illegal drugs trade. This was not only from natural based drugs like heroin but the many manmade creations; these latter being sometimes more dangerous.

Because of his success in his work, he had survived two assassination attempts but these had not deterred him. After Sanchez had waited for about five minutes with increasing impatience the large doors from the office of the Minister opened and a secretary motioned for Sanchez to enter,

"Please come in sir, the Minister is ready now."

Sanchez rose quickly and strode after the secretary. He was surprised to see not just the Minister but a number of people sitting with him at a large round table set in the middle of the wood and marble decorated office.

"Ah, Sanchez, come in," the Minister said with a smile. He then added, "Do sit down there." Indicating a chair facing the Minister and with the other five people round the table. "I expect you are curious as to why you are here."

Sanchez thought, how right you are. I am definitely curious especially with these other people present. The Minister continued, "I will explain, my colleagues sitting here are members of a special committee established by the President of the European Union and are from Germany, France, the UK, Holland, and Belgium." The Minister indicated each member to Sanchez as he went round the table.

"The job of this committee is to establish a new European police force to be known as 'EUDforce.' The 'D' in the middle is to accent the attack on drugs but it is a general Police force as well and will be used for all police matters in the EU. The local police will still operate as usual but the new force will have special powers at present denied to the existing police forces due to human rights legislation. It will act as a coordinating unit in all police matters. An overlay is another way of describing it"

The Minister then paused and continued in an even more serious tone, "The important difference with this force is that it will be able to deal more harshly with all levels of persons in the illegal drugs business. Later, these policies may well extend to other matters. In fact, I am sure this will be the case and soon. However our first main job is illegal drugs." He then went on to give a few examples of what he meant.

"Although drugs will initially be the priority there are other big areas of crime such as the copying of expensive items, and particularly internet crime of many types. Still I repeat, drugs are our top priority."

Sanchez wondered what precisely these various statements meant, especially those about human rights, but he guessed there would be more details later.

The Minister was speaking again. "We are offering you an important position in this force, which we hope you will accept although I realise that the police force here will be very sorry to lose you should you do so. Apart from your excellent work here we are aware that you speak several languages fluently, including English, French and German. These assets would be very useful, as you will see."

Sanchez was hoping the Minister would get to this job offer more quickly although he was not sure he wanted another. While he was thinking, the Minister spoke again.

"The first job of this force, as I have made clear, will be a Europe-wide attack on the drugs trade and we know how keen you are on this issue. We want to interfere drastically with all aspects of illegal drugs, covering the importation, the distribution and use. Now, as to your position..."

Sanchez thought, *at last he is going to tell me.*

After another brief pause the Minister said, "The Chief of this new force has already been chosen. It will be filled by a British man from Scotland Yard a Commander Maurice Talbot."

Sanchez smiled inwardly; he knew Maurice well and had recently been in touch with him over two criminals coming to Madrid. They had come onto his patch, were quickly caught and dispatched to a long prison sentence. Maurice was a good choice as he was extremely effective and was doing a good job in the UK. He had told Sanchez that drugs were also his biggest problem and any plan to beat the people behind them must be a good idea. While considering this he wondered when the Minister would get around to his job offer. He did not have long to wait and was surprised when the Minister said,

"We would like you to be the second-in-command of this new force. However, your first task will be to take close control of setting up the EUDforce in each EU country. I will explain in more detail. We have decided that until we are certain we get the right people you will command the whole anti-drugs unit and then you will pick your successor and the backing staff. We know that you are young and this job will test you. I am sure you will rise to the challenge."

Another pause and then, "Your first country will be the UK as it has one of the highest drug usages. Other countries will follow as soon as you can pick your men. The job you are to do is the most important, but the force will also have its administrative part and another new section dealing with drug rehabilitation. All activities when dealing with countries outside the EU will be handled by the new EU Foreign Office with which you will work when necessary, probably through the Paris headquarters of the new force."

After glancing around the room the minister continued, "There are questions that some members of the committee would like to ask you and I am sure you will have some of your own."

Sanchez thought – I certainly do have quite a lot of questions especially that bit about doing the job country by country; that seems very slow against the apparent urgency indicated by the other comments. However, he was too absorbed in the actual job offer to think more deeply about that aspect of the administration.

Nodding to the members, the Minister indicated that they could start asking any questions. The French representative spoke first. "I've seen all the papers regarding your suitability for this work and I am satisfied as to your abilities but the headquarters will be in France. Are you willing to go there?"

"Yes, that would not be a problem," replied Sanchez, "But there are obviously some questions about the job itself that require further explanation."

The Minister had been looking at his wristwatch and interjected, "I realise there are many questions about the task and I suggest that as the time is right we go to lunch in less formal surroundings and continue there." A secretary opened the doors and the Minister led them all upstairs to a large dining room.

No one noticed one of the secretaries going out of a rear door and slipping into a public phone booth. The phone call was to Germany and it repeated almost word for word what had transpired in the Minister's office. From there it would go to forewarn many high echelons in the drugs business.

Sanchez was having some deep thoughts as he followed the people upstairs. He felt honoured to be chosen for what obviously was going to be a high powered job but he liked his life in Spain. In fact, the more he considered, the more he felt that his present life was quite perfect. He continued to think as he ascended the stairs and the party entered the dining room.

It was very ornate and the table was laid in a manner that caused Sanchez to reflect on how the rich live, but he rapidly decided he would soon grow fed up with this; he liked a more simple life.

He asked and answered many questions while all the committee were having coffee and he was pleased with the session. He thought he understood more about the job. He had not actually agreed to take up the appointment but had promised to give his decision the next morning because the Minister stressed that he had to know, as a matter of urgency.

After a sleep and more thought, Sanchez decided to take a chance and go for the new job. He had nothing really to lose and maybe a new challenge would do him good. He had to admit he would miss Spain a great deal, especially the weather.

He phoned up the Ministry and was connected to the Minister after a short wait. "Good morning Sir. I have decided to accept your job offer."

The Minister was obviously pleased and said, "I am delighted about your decision. I hope your expectations are realised and good luck Sanchez."

Sanchez went back to his office to arrange for his departure to France in a week's time. Most of the week was spent with the man who would replace him and the head of police. Sorting out his apartment did take much time. It was an attractive rented apartment in the centre of Madrid and Sanchez kept the interior very simple. He arranged storage for his furniture and effects and told his landlord that the apartment was now empty.

On Monday morning, a car arrived to take him to Madrid airport, en route for Paris. The car had proceeded about halfway to its destination when Sanchez heard what he thought was backfire from another car. He then realised it was not backfire... Someone was shooting at them!

The driver heard it too and took immediate action.

He increased speed to get away. It became clear a few moments later, that the vehicle from which the shots came had now gone in the opposite direction.

Sanchez sensed a slight pain in his leg and it felt sticky: he realised he had been shot. Rolling up his trouser leg he found that his leg had been nicked by a bullet. It was not serious and he wound a handkerchief round his wound to stem the trickle of blood. Meanwhile his driver was travelling fast, but it soon appeared that only the normal traffic was behind them; no vehicle was following directly.

They reached the airport and Sanchez had a plaster put on his leg by a nurse in the airport *ambulatorio*. He also reported the incident to the police, as did the driver. After signing a brief statement, he went on his way. As Sanchez sat in his aircraft seat on his way to Paris, he pondered on another botched attempt on his life and another lucky escape; the bullet could have killed him. He also wondered how anyone had known of his movements. He would ring the police later and discuss the matter.

The flight was uneventful and after the usual formalities, Sanchez was through customs and into the main hall of 'Charles de Gaulle' airport. A man with a picture of Sanchez and a police identity card was waiting. He looked at a picture as Sanchez came through the arrival doors and moved towards him. He then said,

"Good morning Sir, I have been sent to drive you to the Paris offices, can I take your bag." Sanchez gave him his case and they walked to the car that was parked nearby.

They sped off to the new EUDforce offices in Paris. When they arrived the driver led Sanchez to the reception desk and said, "This man will now take you up to the offices Sir," and handed Sanchez his case. Sanchez thanked him and was then asked by the man at the reception,

"Will you please follow me sir." Sanchez was led to the lift and they travelled to the fifth floor where the receptionist knocked on an office door.

"Come in," said a strong voice and Sanchez walked in to a large bare office with a simple table, a telephone and a few chairs. A tall and well built man with broad shoulders and a smiling face rose to greet Sanchez. "Pedro, jolly good to see you again, there is not much here at the moment as you can see. Anyway come and sit down, would you like a drink?"

Sanchez replied with a grin, "Good to see you too, yes I'd love a coffee."

"Well old boy, that's about all we can get at the moment; it's all happening in a few days time." Talbot rang for coffee for both of them and then told Sanchez what he knew so far. "I'm told that the most important thing is that all the various governments have been told to cooperate with us on pain of being in the dog-house with the Commission and probably fined a hefty amount of Euros."

Sanchez nodded, "That was my concern, that we would have no teeth and be frustrated in the job. What about the overall budget for the new force?"

"Ah, Pedro," replied Talbot, "That is an interesting question. The Chairman of the committee has told me that there is a very large sum of money already earmarked for us.

Europe as a whole has decided that the drugs business must be broken and money is not a problem."

"That sounds very good," said Sanchez." I hope they don't change their minds later as this business is going to take time." He paused for a moment. "What about the budgets of the various countries. We are likely to cause them extra expense, particularly in the early days."

Maurice nodded, "I have been told that this is not our worry either. The committee will sort it out. We report to the Chairman who is our political master."

They continued chatting for a considerable time and agreed the first job was to call the various heads of the police in all the EU countries, introduce themselves and tell them that in a week or so they would arrange a meeting to talk about the overall strategy. Both men were pleased when the Director of administration arrived the following day together with a handful of his key staff. Talbot said with a laugh, "Perhaps we'll get some food organised now."

Within two more days equipment of all kinds arrived and was installed by engineers. So far it was all the usual stuff, computers, video links and loads of standard office equipment. In conversation with Talbot, Sanchez learned that Talbot had been informed that after settling in they could obtain more specialised equipment should they so desire.

The meeting with the police chiefs from the countries forming the European States went fairly well but there were some who thought it might turn out to be a waste of money. The head of the German police was particularly suspicious of the EUDforce and the possibility that his position might be usurped. It took a great deal of persuasion before he saw the advantages.

Some were more enthusiastic because none had overcome the drugs problem alone in their own countries but despite the differences, all wanted to get to grips with the enemy.

The enemy was already thinking about counter measures as the knowledge of this organisation and its aims were already circulating among the drug barons. The battle would soon start and it would be a long and hard one.

4

After the meeting of the Police Chiefs chaired by Maurice Talbot, the German Police Chief went back to his office with mixed emotions. In the majority optimism of the meeting, he had agreed to the general feeling that the EUDforce was a good idea; back in his office, his old doubts returned. He still could not see the reason for another police force and to be fair one or two other Chiefs agreed with him. There was little option for him; the German Government was adamant. The drug trade had to be broken and if this new force was to be the answer then they must subscribe to it in every way.

While the German Policeman was thinking about this, others were also thinking about the new EUDforce. In a small office in a street in Hamburg another meeting was taking place between a different set of Chiefs. Three Germans whose interests and wealth depended on the supply of drugs to German citizens were discussing the message received from the secretary at the Spanish Foreign Office. This secretary could speak German impeccably hence his usefulness there. He had lived in Germany for ten years and had made acquaintance with Franz Werner; who was the leader of the three men.

Werner sat musing for a while then said, "As I see it the only difference will be more police but that's not a problem, we've dealt with that before when the police decided to get more active." He said nothing more for a moment then continued, "On the other hand our weakness might be in our distribution networks, this business of human rights or the lack of them might mean people might talk, or be made to talk"

Another member of the gang interjected, "That's what I think, if the police can do what they like to our distributors they will very likely talk and give the next echelon away. I don't like the sound of it."

The third man sneered at the last speaker, "Getting cold feet already? I think we will be OK; it's all a lot of talk, nothing will happen."

Werner looked at the last speaker and said, "You are very wrong to think this force will make no difference, we must tighten our distribution and weed out any weaklings."

The meeting broke up after more talk about the likely effects of the new police force; none of the three could assess properly what would happen. They agreed to be on their guard. They might have felt easier in their minds had they known that the Commission would take so long in pushing the drugs activity to all countries.

Franz Werner was ruthless in his dealings with any underlings that crossed him or did not perform but he was also capable of clear thinking about his business. He would not have survived so long if he had been otherwise. When he arrived home, he sat and thought more, about the possible future problems that could arise. He concluded that he faced two dangers; the distribution that he had already discussed with the other two drugs operators and the other was the possible curtailment of his supplies.

Werner was a large importer of heroin, bought via intermediaries but he had found out some years ago where a large part of his supplies came from. He contacted the grower; a man called Omar Rahim from time to time and he decided to send a message to him telling him what was going on with this new Police Force. His next move was to think carefully about how much he was isolated from his key distributors.

He had seven, and five of them had no idea from whom they obtained their supplies of drugs. It was all done in a way to avoid leakage of any knowledge of connection with himself.

He felt there was no danger from these five people.

The other two were different; they did know who he was.

This situation had to be remedied; there was only one way to do this, they had to be removed. Werner realised that this should be done as soon as possible; while they lived he was in danger. He knew of course when they were due to receive their next consignment; it would be a good time to eliminate them.

Werner always attended to the handing over of the drugs himself but it was not possible to identify him. He always wrapped up well, with a high coat collar and scarf. He also took care never to handle the goods unless he wore gloves.

His back-up man sat in the van watching over his master.

The first of the two distributors arrived at the meeting place as usual and the exchange was made. Once Werner had the money in his hands he coolly shot the distributor, retrieved the drugs and disappeared as quickly as possible. The speed of this execution and withdrawal from the scene totally surprised the two minders who were supposed to guard the distributor; they looked open-mouthed as Werner disappeared.

The second execution was more difficult; the man did not attend but sent an underling to affect the exchange. A month later a second opportunity occurred and this time it was successful; the distributor was shot dead. However the minder with this distributor was more active and returned fire at Werner who was slightly wounded. His own man finished the job off by shooting the man.

Werner now felt safe, but he had overlooked the obvious: the people who worked closely with him. There were the two men who assisted him at exchanges and watched over him and four others who collected and sorted the drugs.

Messages sent to the remaining distributors saying that more was expected of them, since two of their number were no longer active. They should also ensure that their sub-distributors had no knowledge of them. He told them to get rid of anyone who might give them away to the authorities. He also emphasised the necessity of making sure that it was difficult for any layer of distribution to know the details of the next layer above. He realised that although this sounded easy to say it might be more difficult in practice.

Werner's turnover of money was very large and he had a good way of dealing with it. He ran a popular casino and restaurant not far from the waterfront. It was easy to launder the drugs money in the casino and so far, it seemed that he was above suspicion by the law. The law, however, was not as oblivious to the casino as Werner thought and certain detectives were suspicious.

These men had tried to investigate the business that Werner operated so successfully but they came up with a blank every time. They remained suspicious, but with no evidence they could do nothing.

5

Omar Rahim, whose nephew Hamid lived in Meyhabul, sat in his leather chair in his luxuriously furnished library and private study. He pondered for a few minutes over the information he had received from a contact in Germany. The message was all about the meeting that had taken place between Pedro Sanchez and the Foreign Minister. The uncle was known to most of the people who knew him as Omar Rahim but he had several aliases, which he used when dealing with certain drug contacts.

He grew very large amounts of opium poppies from which he first obtained the opium and then, by various chemical processes, produced heroin. He was a tall man, well built with a face that could change in an instant from apparent good humour to a cruel one. He had streaks of grey in his hair and a short moustache. His general appearance was military and although he had never been in any military service he ran his whole drugs operation in an efficient military style and showed no mercy to anyone he felt was not working hard enough. He was capable of murder at a whim; no record existed of the employees that simply disappeared.

He employed about one hundred men to do his bidding and all were frightened of him. They had come to work there, thinking that they were going to work for a reasonable man;

unfortunately, they found themselves trapped in a life of misery. The wages were minimal and food was not very plentiful. They were treated more like slaves than human beings.

Omar continued to study the information he had received and when he had finished reading he called in his estate manager and handed him the written copy of the message. Ahmed, the estate manager, was the opposite of his employer in appearance and demeanour. He was a thin man, not very tall, a pale complexion and thinning hair. He was an accountant and looked after all the administration of the estate. This he did in a very efficient manner making sure that his master was well protected by the bribes he paid and that the accounts recorded every detail. Ahmed never disclosed what he thought about the activities on the estate so he was an ideal person to do his master's bidding.

He was the only person that Omar ever really took into his confidence, and against all the previous statements about Omar's character, he probably would never have harmed his manager. This assumption was not just due to the excellent way Ahmed, the manager, performed his duties – there was a closeness between the two men.

"What do you make of that, Ahmed?" asked Omar as he handed him the message.

His manager read the paper and looked up, "It seems more definite than some warnings we have received but I doubt that anything much will come of it." He looked at the message again, "The Europeans have been trying to get their act together for many years but have never managed it yet."

Omar considered Ahmed's answer for a moment then said, "What about the British involvement? They have never shown much interest in joining into European affairs before but now they have. Is that not significant?"

Ahmed laughed. "I don't think they will make much difference." Ahmed did not know how wrong he was in his analysis of the situation, but time would reveal the truth; it might not be pleasant for either of them.

Ahmed knew all about the drugs operation, he had been with Omar when they had started. He was the soul of discretion and although he felt sorry for the people that disappeared, he was utterly faithful to Omar. He did not look after any part of the opium production except the accounting. While Omar Rahim lived in his large mansion with its many hectares of land, stables for his fine horses and an aura of luxury throughout, the actual drugs operation was carried out several kilometres away in a shallow valley. Near to this, in three large fields of many hectares, the poppies were grown.

The location was ideal for the work that went on in there and, very conveniently, the aircraft runway ran the whole length of the valley. Also in the valley was a row of rough wooden huts where the workers lived in conditions that were terrible, while Omar lived in luxury in his mansion.

None of Omar's activity would have been possible without the cooperation of individuals in high places. Coercion might be a better word than cooperation because most were frightened what might happen to them if they did not do as they were asked. Corruption was rife and it spread downwards to the lower ranks, so Omar was left strictly alone to pursue his evil activities and increase his bank balance.

One unfortunate official, who did object to what was going on, was never seen again. A police officer, brave enough to question the activity of the valley and who endeavoured to look around the estate, was found nearby in the surrounding countryside, with his throat cut and all his clothes removed.

Men selected by Rahim to protect him and his property guarded the whole area carefully day and night. These men were loyal, provided their excellent pay continued. They were ruthless and any stranger straying near would receive no mercy. There was no finesse about the chemical processes carried out to produce the morphine and then heroin; all was done in old cooking pots, old oil drums and rough barbeque-like heating stoves. It was a vast business and no one was allowed to interfere with it.

Omar spoke to his manager, "I'm going to the valley Ahmed. I want to see how soon the next load will be ready. It should have been today but I have not had a call yet from the foreman." Ahmed nodded and carried on with his accounts; he felt sorry for the foreman if anything was wrong, as he knew how ruthless his master could be.

Omar drove up to the valley in his Mercedes overland vehicle, similar to a large Range Rover and entered the valley to find the place in some uproar. He immediately sought out Mohammed, the foreman of the processing unit, and questioned him about the noise. Mohammed explained that when the present load was checked, ready for transportation, there was a quantity missing. "We are trying to find out when it could have been stolen. We have never had such a problem before," he said in a faltering voice.

Omar's face became set in stone and Mohammed was frightened. He knew what his master was capable of doing. There followed a thorough investigation but, with no ready explanation, Omar said finally, "You will find out the answer by tomorrow morning, or you will suffer."

Mohammed worried throughout the night and talked to all his colleagues but could not discover how the heroin might have disappeared. Early in the morning, as soon as it was light, he stole away quietly from the valley. He took a little food and a small bottle of water and went into the comforting undulating countryside: he hoped no one would find him.

After travelling for what seemed an interminable distance he felt exhausted and had to rest. He slept for a few hours, then travelled on towards the border with Pakistan.

The next morning at about seven thirty Omar arrived back in the valley. He looked for Mohammed but to no avail, then was told that the foreman had gone. He had stolen away sometime before work started. Omar was furious, how dare this speck of humanity thwart him by going, he would send trackers and dogs after him but first he determined to find out about the missing heroin. He questioned everyone again and decided that a man who had recently come to work for him was the likely culprit. He had the frightened individual brought before him. The man had some inkling of what might befall him from listening to stories told to him by the other workers. He said in a quivering voice, "I have not stolen anything, I have not done anything." He looked up at Omar and his face was white as the lime which they used in the chemical processes.

Omar completely ignored the protestations, calmly took out his revolver and shot him. "Bury him," Omar Rahim ordered, "If I have any more trouble I will shoot the lot of you." The men cowered away and did as they were told.

Omar drove back to his mansion and arranged for dogs and trackers to set off to find Mohammed. They returned three days later saying there was no trail they could follow. It grew fainter out in the countryside and there were too many directions to follow. "What about the dogs, could they not get a scent," Rahim demanded.

"It appears not Sir, there were several streams in which Mohammed could have travelled and the dogs lost the scent." This news increased Omar's anger but there was little he could do. If he killed too many of his workers he could not continue. He chose his fastest horse and rode all out round the estate to reduce his anger.

When he came back from his ride he went straight to the valley to supervise the first stage of the heroin's transportation. He realised the load was now late, which might cause problems with the buyer, but hell ...the buyer was not always on time himself. This thought helped to dull his anger.

The pilot of the aeroplane was not as frightened of him as were the other men, he knew Omar would have difficulty in replacing him, but even so, he remained wary of his master. The heroin was loaded onto a plane standing ready on the runway and the pilot and Omar went aboard.

They flew south, to a remote corner of Afghanistan near the Pakistan border where, if all went well, they would meet the men who would buy their load. There were other routes through Russia but the buyers had always found the present way marginally safer. No route was safe in the full sense, as there was a real possibility of losing the heroin through robbery or even being killed. There were many enemies: the authorities, natural hazards, brigands or double crossing by other buyers.

Omar and his pilot arrived at the appointed place, they had brought food and drink with them and all they could do was wait for a buyer to arrive. Mobile phones did not operate well in the area. Omar knew he was late and it was possible that he had missed a buyer.

They ate some food and drank water while they waited. Six hours after their arrival – it was nearly nightfall, when they heard noises up the trail; they hoped this was their contact. While Omar and the pilot were waiting, another seller – this time with mules, came to sell a load of heroin.

Omar knew the man and had met him from time to time but never engaged in much conversation with him. He preferred to keep his own counsel, as the least said the better.

Within a short while a group of men with mules came over the border and the leader came up to Omar. "We meet again my friend, I am afraid we are very late this time."

In reply, Omar said, "We were late ourselves so it is fortunate for both of us."

"How much have you brought this time?" asked the buyer.

"Enough to satisfy you I think."

The buyer and Omar examined the load together, with the buyer weighing it and testing various samples, "You have fifty-five kilos, at a street value today of about three and a quarter million dollars. Shall we say two hundred thousand dollars?"

This was always the game. Omar felt he should get much more, but if this buyer did not take it he would have to try the Russian buyers and they were not at all generous. He knew there were many stages in the buying and selling of the heroin but he wanted as big a share as possible. "What about two hundred and fifty thousand?" Omar asked.

"Oh no, I would not be able to sell it on with that purchase price, there are too many people wanting a share on the way to the final customer," replied the buyer, "I have many problems in shipping this stuff and my buyers want to pay as little as possible." He paused for a moment. "I will be very generous, say two hundred and five thousand dollars?"

Omar tried for more but finally accepted the price. He also knew that other man-made drugs were being sold in large quantities so maybe the amount was not too bad and it was in dollars. The money was handed over to Omar in US currency and the buyer departed. The pilot turned their plane and they were soon away, heading back to the valley.

The buyer was right in saying that the journey was hard; it was long and very hazardous and the delivery was uncertain. There were several buyers on this trail and all were the same when it came to price. Again, corruption went hand in hand with the journey.

Two events unknown to Omar at this time were to play an important part in his life. One was the fate of his previous foreman, Mohammed. Fifteen days after he had left the valley to escape from Omar Rahim he staggered into a village in Pakistan. He was emaciated and very weak. He slept for nearly two days after being fed and clothed by the villagers. He had no idea that within a year he would be quite famous.

The other event would be a meeting by Omar with his nephew, who certainly was the farthest thought from his mind at this time. He was thinking more about how his wealth was accumulating. He had succeeded up to now in getting his money to a western bank to make sure that one day he would retire to even more luxury, probably somewhere in the West.

Many years ago, the moneylender had laid out all the procedures to enable the money to be banked in a western bank. Omar did not know how it worked but it did and, of course, there was a cost; Omar suspected that the moneylender still profited from this cost. Omar reflected that he should not mind this as the money was accumulating nicely.

Fate however has a habit of upsetting the best-laid plans but Omar could not imagine any change that would upset his comfortable life.

6

A senior officer from Scotland Yard met Sanchez when he flew to Heathrow and a car was waiting outside the terminal to take him to a first face-to-face meeting with the head of Scotland Yard. The Commissioner had been well briefed by the Home Office, on how he should deal with the EUDforce. The central message was that he must give all the help he could to Sanchez. Privately the Commissioner was not happy about this new police force but decided he had better cooperate.

The Commissioner received Sanchez courteously. After a general conversation, he asked Sanchez, "What sort of help can I give you?"

Sanchez replied, "There are two initial tasks I have to achieve. One is to set up an intelligence task force, the other is to recruit immediately, sixty senior people, or people that are ready for promotion. They will be Chief Superintendents, Superintendents or Chief Inspectors. These people will be in charge of the individual sites. I then want to send them on a course in France. This will be organised by the Paris HQ."

"By my old friend Maurice Talbot?"

Sanchez acknowledged this with a nod and a smile. He then spoke again, "I might send the intelligence people later but I need them to start immediately. I have to get all the information I can about the general drug situation in the UK. Perhaps we can discuss this first?"

The Commissioner thought for a moment then said, "I think you are aware that although we have a central drugs unit at the Yard there are units in each of the Provincial forces. I think it might be unwise to touch the central unit but draw your team from the County forces. I agree that perhaps one or two people that are more experienced could be included from the Yard. It will be easier for us to work together."

Sanchez replied, "I agree, that seems a good compromise, as long as we get a few experienced men or women." The Commissioner asked how many staff Sanchez might need. He replied that about thirty people would do for a start. "I am sure that later we may recruit people ourselves but we need experience now."

The Commissioner said, "If you can give me a few days I can get in touch with all the Chief Constables and I am sure we can get the relevant staff together here for interviews. I will get people for the drug intelligence unit first, and what about the sixty other staff? Would you like some of them to be people who currently work in drugs units?"

Sanchez replied, "That would be fine. It also might help to avoid too much drain on the other areas of the police." He then thought for a moment, "It is not essential of course for all of them. I am happy to leave the selection to you. There is one other matter, which would be very helpful. I could do with a small office where I could have a few staff and a good administrator to help with some of the chores. It will be a while before I get our London site"

"That's no problem Pedro, I'll get something organised for you. As it happens I know of a bright young administrator and staffing the office will be easy."

Sanchez thanked the Commissioner and turned to go when the Commissioner said, "Oh, Pedro, one question before you go. There is a lot of talk among the ranks, wondering how you expect to succeed when we find it difficult to get information from the lower echelons in the drugs racket."

"I can understand that. The answer is in the freedom we shall have to hold and question people and also bend some of the human rights laws. There will be no magistrates and lawyers to interfere"

The Commissioner raised his eyebrows, nodded and said, "I see, well that is a big problem and if you can manage to get over that I wish you luck."

Sanchez replied, "Well, I don't think it is all going to depend on human rights or the lack of them but I hope it will help. After a more general conversation, Sanchez said, "I have to be off now. I have a lot of work to do getting premises throughout the country. Fortunately Government assistance is available to help me."

"As a matter of interest how many sites are you planning to have?" asked the Commissioner.

"We have estimated that thirty sites will be sufficient," replied Sanchez. He then said goodbye, and left the office. His next appointment was with a Government Minister.

"Good afternoon Pedro, nice to meet you; I hope we will be able to help you."
"I hope so and thank you for seeing me so promptly."

The Minister then asked, "Perhaps you can tell me exactly what you need." Sanchez explained what he required and the Minister promised to help to obtain suitable buildings within a few weeks. Some would be temporary and most would require alteration but it would enable things to start.

As Sanchez had not eaten a proper meal since he arrived in the UK he decided to go to his hotel, change and have a meal. He rang Maurice Talbot on his mobile just to tell him that things were going well and that the Commissioner had been very helpful. Privately he was thinking how different things were now the EU had made this important decision. Previously it would have been impossible to do what he was about to start. Making his way to his hotel he was conscious of someone following him and tried to evade this unwelcome attention, but to no avail. He reached the hotel without incident but he wondered who it was and why the interest.

The next morning, after breakfast, Sanchez rang Talbot again to ask when the training course would be ready because the Commissioner had been in touch to say that in spite of objections from a few Chief Constables, recruiting was going well. Five days after seeing the Commissioner, Sanchez was told that sixty men and women would be available for interview. A hotel room had already been booked together with rooms for the recruits to stay until they moved to Paris for the course.

The entrances were guarded by two constables; what Sanchez had to say was not something he wanted the general public to know, at least not yet. However, he was under no illusion that secrecy could be kept for long. Sanchez asked each candidate a series of questions that he and Talbot had prepared including concerns about losing rank but not salary, being prepared to go anywhere at a moment's notice, and willingness to sign a contract with the new organisation.

Sanchez then came on to the subject of human rights. He asked, "What are your thoughts about the human rights laws? In certain circumstances, would you be willing to bend or ignore the human rights legislation? Are you willing to sign the Official Secrets Act if you have not done so already?"

The interviews lasted nearly two days. At the end he had picked forty-seven men and eight women. This was five short of his original aim but he decided not to delay further.

When all the interviews were completed, the recruits gathered in the large room and he addressed the successful men and women. "Thank you all for coming and for going through the interview process. You have been successful and will go on a two-week course to France. I know that you have all signed the   Official Secrets Act but I want you to sign a new one which is with the papers in front of you. This has a specific section on the EUDforce. You also have the contract of employment to sign. I have arranged for police union officials to help you in case there is something you are concerned about. However, I believe you will find the contract of employment very straightforward. I'll leave you for an hour or so while you go through the papers."

When Sanchez returned he found no problems and all had signed the papers. Talbot and the Paris administrator had prepared the straightforward, simple document and it was not expected to cause much difficulty. Before he spoke Sanchez dismissed the police union officials and made sure that the doors were closed and guarded from outside.,

"I am glad you have all signed the new O.S.A. as I can now tell you what is not specifically mentioned in this contract. If there is anyone who cannot agree to my next statement he or she can leave but remember you have signed the O.S.A. I have been authorised by the EU committee that on certain occasions we can ignore the human rights laws and can detain people for almost as long as we like. There will be no lawyers or magistrates involved unless we ask for them. You will recall that I mentioned this briefly during your interview."

He then gave examples of where this could occur. "For example if we or the British police know about a person who is peddling drugs but will not tell who their supplier is we give them two choices. One is to tell and we may help them with a new identity if necessary and if they give us enough information. Alternatively, we threaten to send them to a prison in Belgium for a very long time. This prison has been specially prepared for us. We hope this procedure will change minds. There will be similar instances, when choices might be offered but in each case the head of the EUDforce station will always make the final decision."

Sanchez paused and then asked, "Is anyone not happy with this?" There was silence for a moment or two with people looking at one another. One of the women put her hand up...

"I don't think I can agree with this so I am afraid I cannot join this organisation. I am sorry to have wasted your time"

Sanchez replied, "I can understand your sentiments and respect them. Please remember that you have signed the Official Secrets Act and good luck to you. We are going to finish shortly and then you can get your expenses to date from the office. The administrator will settle up all hotel bills and the rest of you will go home until the end of this week. You have three days to sort out your affairs. You will report here on Monday, and on Tuesday, you will go to Paris for two weeks special training. I shall see you on your return."

While the recruits were in France, Sanchez was very busy. He had heard from the Minister that the search for premises was going well. With the specifications, which Sanchez had supplied to the Minister. Sanchez decided that he would concentrate on the site in London in order to make an early start on testing the system. In any case, the London site would become the headquarters in the UK. He and the administrator looked at the site in the city, chosen by the Minister's people. It was an old warehouse and suited the plan to have first some temporary accommodation. The final build could proceed while they were getting on with their anti-drugs work.

The Minister had found a reputable builder who had carried out government work before and easily understood what was required.

Before he had left Paris, Talbot and Sanchez designed a cells unit in which to keep prisoners. After being constructed in France, the first one would be shipped over, to be fitted onto the London site, so Sanchez left the administrator to attend to the contracts etc. and decided to fly to Paris to see Talbot. On his way Sanchez had a few brief moments of doubt; in a short time, the real business would begin and they had to deliver results.

He thought about the fact that the theories behind this organisation were all untested. All the expectations of the EU depended on the project working and justifying the major expenditure. He then thought, but I'm expected to make it work and I will. He wondered about the person who followed him back to his hotel. Nothing significant had happened so maybe it was not worth thinking about any more.

With more pleasant thoughts in his head and the drone of the aircraft, he drifted off to sleep for twenty minutes. If he could have looked into the future, he might not have gone to sleep so easily. This job was going to test Sanchez to the limit. No bending of human rights legislation would provide all the answers. The drug barons and their hirelings would not give in easily.

7

Omar Rahim was not particularly happy. Delivering more heroin, on his last journey, he had learned that the buyers were getting very jumpy and wanted to pay less than ever. Two things had happened. Firstly the Pakistan authorities had a blitz on the buyers and this made them nervous. In terms of the amount of heroin seized the total was not large but the buyers obviously did not like it: a good excuse to pay less. Omar wished he could get more dollars but the buyers were cautious.

Secondly, and perhaps more importantly, there had been an unexpected fall in the street price of heroin. On his last trip with fifty kilos, the street price was twenty dollars a gram. Omar received an even smaller price for his efforts and pondered over other ways of moving it. In the past, he had thought of trying to fly the heroin to a ship well out in the Arabian Sea. He would need a bigger plane to do this and might not be able to fly over Pakistan.

He approached a friend in the Afghan military with whom he had done business before. They talked about the possibilities. "Would it be possible?" asked Omar.

"No chance Omar, the Pakistan Air Force would not give you permission and to try it without, well they would be on to you immediately. I think it would be suicide."

Omar thought hard and long about this conversation and reluctantly concluded that he would be mad to try. There was the Russian route but this was even longer and generally more expensive, and certainly not any safer than Pakistan. The whole problem was the number of people who had a slice of the money on the way to the final consumer.

A month later Omar was again moving heroin on the old route as no alternative seemed possible when on the return flight he felt a slight pain in his chest. He thought he should not have hurried his food while waiting for the buyer and soon settle down when his chest felt better. When he arrived home he had a meeting with Ahmed, his estate manager and asked if all was well in the valley.

"Well no, I am afraid that we have lost several workmen."

This information was like a red rag to a bull as far as Omar was concerned. His face turned very ugly and he stormed out to his car and drove at speed to the valley. Again, he felt a slight pain in his chest but it passed quickly. His entrance to the valley was greeted with trepidation by the remaining workmen: they knew how ruthless he could be. The man whom Omar had made foreman after Mohammed had absconded, was very frightened to see Omar hurrying towards him.

Omar shouted at the unfortunate man, "What is the explanation for these people leaving?"

"They went at night Sir. No one saw them go." Omar was very angry but there was no excuse to shoot this wretch of a foreman, he needed him at the moment. There was no doubt that the fault lay with his guards so he turned abruptly and strode off to the first of the guards on the edge of the valley.

He felt the tightening in his chest again, but after pausing briefly the feeling passed and he strode on towards the guard and harangued him about the missing workmen. The guards were not as frightened as the other workers were but this guard should have been more wary.

Omar said, "Why have you allowed workmen to leave? I pay you to stop then."

The guard replied, "Wait a bit, I can't see in the dark, anyway you have plenty more left, what is the problem?" This insolent reply increased Omar's anger; how dare this insolent slob speak to him like that. It was all Omar needed to get his gun out of his pocket and prepare to shoot. The guard, seeing Omar drawing the gun, said loudly,

"Steady on, there are others besides me, I'm not to blame." Omar's steely smile was set in his face of stone as he pointed the gun at the guard. "No, no, you can't do that, please no," The guard realised too late that Omar was definitely going to shoot him. His cries for mercy had no effect on Omar as he aimed his revolver and without any further hesitation shot the guard between the eyes.

After this act, Omar's anger abated slightly and he went to the head guard farther up the valley and told him that the same fate would befall him, unless security was improved. Every one hated Omar but, because of the good money he paid, the head guard was very polite and promised that nothing like this would ever happen again. As Omar turned away he said, "You know what will happen if it does."

He returned to his house and consulted Ahmed about the slight pain and discomfort he suffered from time to time. Ahmed was sympathetic and suggested that Omar should see a doctor in case there was a problem. When Omar rejected the idea Ahmed shrugged his shoulders and repeated,

"Well I think you should see a doctor, I am sure all is ok but why not do it." Omar demurred again but eventually Ahmed persuaded him and he called his doctor who he came out to examine him. After a thorough and detailed examination the doctor said,

"I have a good idea what might be wrong but I would like you to go to the hospital for some tests that I cannot do here."

"What do you think the problem is then?" Omar asked.

The doctor hesitated for a moment then replied, "I have given you many tests and it is difficult to be sure without the hospital analysis. I think you may have a narrowing of the aortic valve. This may well get worse if there is calcification there. The hospital tests will tell me more. If I am correct, the answer will be a new heart valve. You would have to go to the West to get such an operation carried out. It could not be done here with any chance of success; in fact I think it would be impossible. I can advise you further after the tests."

A week later, after tests at the hospital, the doctor came again to see Omar. "My preliminary diagnosis seems correct. With the equipment available at the hospital, they tell me that the problem is almost certainly the valve. The next thing would be to see a surgeon in the West, who can give you more comprehensive tests than we can, but I think the answer is clear." After the doctor went, for the first time in his life, Omar suddenly felt alone and a little frightened. Ahmed was all right but Omar's realisation went deeper, there was no family.

He thought about this for some time then suddenly realised there was some family after all. He had a nephew, Hamid, living in a town called Meyhabul. Yes of course he remembered his nephew Hamid. He had not seen him for a very long time. A few moments later Omar recovered his composure but the thought of his nephew remained. He would ask him to come soon for a holiday; it would be good to see him again.

As the weeks passed, Omar managed to sell the rest of his heroin stocks and new crops were planted. He had some pain in his chest and got out of breath but provided he did not exert himself, it was not a great problem. One day the thought of his nephew again came into his mind and he decided to write to him. The letter was brief and said,

"Hamid, I have not seen you for a very long time, would you like to visit me soon? I have enclosed money for your fare. Let me know when you are coming and I will arrange for a car to meet you at the bus station." He sent Ahmed to town with the letter to post and life went on as usual although something felt different to Omar: something he could not explain.

All the crops were planted, and the usual crop of maize grown as well, to keep the weeds down. New chemicals were brought in, ready for the processes that would turn the opium into heroin.

Hamid liked his job in the town of Meyhabul and the moneylender had congratulated him on the way he carried out his duties. There were no bad payers; Hamid had persuaded all the debtors to pay up at the proper time. Hamid had been thinking about the letter he received from his Uncle and he read it again. He talked with his wife about accepting the offer of a visit to his uncle. She said, "Think carefully before you go, I really don't want you to leave."

Hamid did think about it but curiosity won the day and he told his wife that he had decided to go. He wrote to his uncle thanking him for the invitation and the fare; the next morning he saw the moneylender. He was sorry to hear that Hamid was leaving but understood the reasoning behind the decision.

He warned Hamid again about his uncle and told him to be careful. "Come and see me when you return as I want you back in your job."

Hamid felt both guilty and pleased that he was wanted; in his previous jobs the employer could not have cared less.

Meanwhile Omar Rahim did not know why he felt eager to see his nephew. He asked Ahmed every day whether a letter had come from Hamid; Ahmed saw a distinct change in Omar's personality at least where his nephew was concerned. Omar still suffered from discomfort in his chest and he noticed that he soon got out of breath when walking.

Three weeks later a letter arrived and Omar saw that Hamid would arrive in three days time. At last, the day dawned and Omar with Ahmed and a driver went to the bus station to meet his nephew. Hamid arrived hot and stiff from his journey; the roads were rough and the bus was old. That combination produced a bone-shaking ride and Hamid was very pleased to get off. His uncle strode to meet him and they shook hands. Hamid was a little shy but managed a smile and answered his uncle's questions about his journey. He was introduced to Ahmed and the three men walked to the car to drive back to the estate.

Hamid was overawed when he saw his uncle's home and they all talked until late into the night. Ahmed was amazed at the change in Omar; he seemed a different person once the nephew had arrived. He even talked to some of the workmen as though they were human beings instead of the low-life he usually considered them. Hamid lost all sense of time and while he wrote occasionally to his wife, it was many weeks before he considered whether he should return.

His wife had asked several times about this, but Hamid was learning so much about the heroin business that he was getting used to being there. His uncle had not indicated that he should leave: rather, he seemed pleased for Hamid to stay. Omar paid Hamid so that he could send money to his wife but while his wife was glad of the money she wondered about Hamid's return. By now in fact, Hamid was doing a lot of the supervisory work and relieving his uncle of many tasks. Hamid wondered about the moneylender and his warning regarding his uncle. Why had the warning had been given? He saw no dangers in his life on the estate.

The dangers were building many hundreds of kilometres away but Hamid was totally unaware of such matters.

The sun was shining and life was good.

8

Sanchez arrived in Paris a few days before the special training for his recruits was completed. He saw his boss, Maurice Talbot, and was amazed at the transformation of the EUDforce offices in such a short time. They were now starting to buzz with information from all the EU countries.

The new force would eventually cooperate with and coordinate all EU policing, as the original plan demanded. This did not mean that local police forces were non-existent but they would operate under the umbrella of EUDforce. There were many staff operating computers and the video links were beginning to function. It helped a great deal when the people could see each other; facial expressions said a lot in a conversation.

Sanchez could see that once the HQ was up to full potential information would flow rapidly in the whole system. This gave the new force a distinct edge over the previous slow collaboration. He thought about Villains, they were getting smarter and quicker all the time so this rapid interchange of information was essential.

The problem that he saw was the ability of the staff to manage the vast flows of information that would exist. The carefully chosen staff would have to be people of the highest calibre. He would mention this to Talbot.

Talbot greeted Sanchez warmly and asked for the latest update on work in London, and enquired how the workforce was settling down. Sanchez said things were going well, the temporary part of the London premises was virtually complete and the custom-built holding cells would be in position in two to three days.

By the time the whole building was finished, in two months time, their communication system would connect fully with the Paris HQs and to the UK police database. He also added that he was looking forward to starting the real work.

He mentioned the problem regarding information flowing in the new system. Talbot agreed, "I have asked a top university professor in Germany in the field of information flow, to write a job specification for the post; the existing staff are temporary although some may be ok. We shall see when we interview everyone under the new specifications"

They continued to talk for nearly two hours and Talbot told Sanchez about progress at headquarters. The experience in London would be very valuable to set a pattern for the rest of the sites in the UK and indeed all the EU countries.

Sanchez then went to the training camp where his team members were busy. They had been educated for the first days on how to keep fit. They were not going to be athletes overnight, but a degree of fitness was necessary. The next sessions were to teach them awareness and the ability to follow people without giving themselves away.

Another series of workshops taught them how interviewing should be carried out; it included a few exercises ignoring human rights. Sanchez sat in on some of the lectures and participated in the arts of following people. He realised there was quite a lot he had never practised himself; he hoped he could leave that to others. The final part of the course was the recognition of the most common drugs with which they would come in contact.

He could see that the two weeks were being very useful to his people and looked forwards to getting the results of the individual participants.

Before the course ended, he went back to London to make sure that the building work was proceeding properly. He found the administrator on the London site with the builder and things were going extremely well. Sanchez examined carefully the first holding cells received from France, as without these he could not bring anyone in for questioning. They would be ready on time, as promised. The Paris HQ assured him that further cells would be available when he wanted them. There was enough work done, for Sanchez to believe that the main work would proceed on time.

On the Monday following his return from France, his team of men and women arrived from their intensive course and assembled in one of the temporary offices where Sanchez discussed with them their time in France and what they had learned. When the discussion ended, Sanchez spoke about the jobs they had to do soon. "There is no other site as ready as this one so I have decided that we all work here for the time being." He then updated them on other preparations. "More sites will follow in about two weeks and then they can be manned."

Sanchez spoke about the methods they would have to adopt. "There will be drug peddlers, caught by the police and brought here for questioning. We will then see if there are flaws in the main theory, that our ability to do things not allowed to the police will be helpful. We need to get the simple peddlers to tell us who supplies them. We then need to get them to tell us who they supply and so on up the chain. It will not be as easy as I have made it sound but that is our goal. The hardest task will be to move up to the big boys and stop them. This is the theory; we have to make it work in practice."

To cover three eight-hour shifts, the total number of staff was split into three. Sanchez hoped that the participants would shared experiences. When the other sites were ready, he hoped these senior staff would slot into place immediately. They could then educate their backing staff.

While they waited for the cells to be ready Sanchez held workshops on various aspects of how he thought they might proceed; he was pleased by the good brain-storming sessions. He had already set up the intelligence team in one of the temporary offices; all their equipment computers were tied into the site network as well as each other.

The cells were now ready and Sanchez was anxious to start. They were designed so that no prisoner could see another and interview rooms were nearby. The plan was to increase the cells with another batch of six in the final build. London was a big city; they would have to deal with a large area. They would also have to ensure a rapid turnaround of captives, otherwise the number of cells would never be enough.

On the following Wednesday, the local police brought in two people who had been caught selling drugs and, as usual, had refused to give any information about their suppliers. They were put into separate cells at the EUDforce station, until the next morning. Sanchez arrived bright and early and asked the duty sergeant if the two people had eaten breakfast.

"One has, Sir, but the other one is being awkward."

"Right," said Sanchez, "I'll deal with the awkward squad first." Accompanied by four of his staff, he found a young man in a truculent mood, who would not give his name or age.

"Well now," said Sanchez, "I understand you won't tell us your name." The man just looked at Sanchez in an insolent fashion and said nothing. "You have two choices," said Sanchez solemnly, "Either you tell me all that I want to know or you go to prison for thirty years in a very unpleasant prison in Belgium."

The man looked up at this and said, "...'Nar', I'll get the usual, just a warning from the magistrate."

"I'm afraid, young man, that's where you're wrong. You will see no magistrate or solicitor action in this force. Now I'll ask you again, firstly your name and age?" The man was obviously pondering on Sanchez's statement but still did not believe him. Sanchez waited a few moments and then said, "There is a van waiting outside to take you to prison for thirty years. I will give you one more minute to answer me or off you go and I assure you the prison is not like the ones here; no television or games, just hard labour."

The man was weighing up what Sanchez had said but still could not believe that it could happen. It had never been like this before. "Ok," said Sanchez firmly, "You've had your minute so off you go." He called two of his men and told them to take the man to the waiting van. They had nearly got to the van when the man suddenly shouted out.

"No, I don't want to go to prison; I'll tell you my name."

The men holding him brought him back to Sanchez where, reluctantly, the man gave his name and age. "Fine," said Sanchez, "Now I want to know where you live." Again very reluctantly the man answered with his address in the East End of London and Sanchez ordered two of his staff to check out the address and see that it was genuine. He cautioned the man, "If you have given me false information then you know where you will go,"

The man said, "Its ok I promise." The next question was more difficult as he was asked who supplied his drugs. He looked very frightened and did not want to answer. "No I can't say that, I might get beaten up or killed."

"Ok," Sanchez responded, "I have no time to waste, you're off to prison."

"No, no, I can't do that t, it would kill me. I have a wife."

"You had a choice, you have chosen prison," Sanchez spoke coldly. The man was crying now and finally gave the name and address of his supplier and with a moan said,

"They will get me I am sure."

The second peddler was much easier to deal with and this time told one of the Chief Superintendents all he wanted to know. Later the CS turned to Sanchez and said, "We would never have got information in the normal way but I wonder, how long before some busy body finds out what we do?"

"My thoughts exactly," relied Sanchez, "but we have the power of the EU behind us." The local police were informed about both suppliers and the places raided.

Many drugs were seized and two suppliers were brought to Sanchez for further interrogation. The local police dealt with the two peddlers. They were charged, but released later, after a small fine. Before they went, Sanchez warned about what they could expect if they sold drugs again or spoke about their experiences in the EUDforce station.

One of the peddlers went back to his small terraced house and saw his partner, a blonde woman with few graces. "I 'gotta' get a job somehow," the peddler said. The girl laughed,

"You never had a job in your life, what's up with you?"

The peddler did not answer, he was thinking of thirty years of hard labour.

The suppliers were in cells and Sanchez said, "Let us see what these two can tell us," The first job was to find out as much as possible about their customers. One of the Chief Superintendents started on this job and Sanchez said, "I want to get to the bigger boys as soon as possible."

He was thinking that this was going to be a long, hard job. He had no idea as to how hard or how long it would really turn out to be.

There were hundreds if not thousands of opium growers. Making it more difficult for them to distribute their evil to Europe, it would deal them a major blow. This then was the hope; remove the route to the customer and the business fails.

Would it work? That was the question.

9

Sanchez left a couple of his staff to deal with the two suppliers and went to see the Minister about the progress of the other sites. The Minister was not available but the man who was chasing things for him assured Sanchez that progress was good. He then talked to the intelligence team and, from work already in progress, learned that they had identified three dealers well up the chain of supply. Having ascertained that steps were in hand to find their customers and suppliers, he left them to carry on with their work. He was pleased that results were beginning to appear.

When he returned to the main office, there were developments in the case of the two detained suppliers. The first man decided to tell his interrogators where he obtained his supplies and the local police were following up on the information. The other man had proved difficult at first but later revealed his source; it was the same supplier as the first detainee had given. Sanchez was disappointed that they were the same, but acknowledged that at least it was some success.

The next job was to find the customers supplied by these men and, after a little delay, Sanchez received the lists. Every supplier listed would be caught and interrogated. They would receive a simple warning before being charged in the Magistrate's court: any further criminal activity after release from prison would result in a very long term in the EUDforce prison in Belgium.

This was now a standard message to all released peddlers and suppliers, and all those put in prison through the EUDforce activity.

The main supplier revealed by the two detainees was never caught; his premises were virtually empty and only a very small quantity of drugs recovered. While Sanchez wondered how the supplier had wind of a possible raid, he was sanguine about the affair. He thought that all the evidence showed that there were hundreds more opportunities for finding fruitful chains of suppliers and drugs. Perhaps he would have thought differently if he had known just how many more there were.

Five more peddlers were detained in the next week and three suppliers identified from their information. Sanchez joined in raids on two of the premises and wished he had not gone on the second. The first raid was a text book operation; two men and one woman were detained and sent to the EUDforce site for grilling.

In the second raid, the police met considerable resistance; firearms were used against them and an armed response unit was called in. The police in their usual way, burst into the house early one morning to catch anyone on the premises. It was not long before the sound of gunfire was heard and the police took cover until the armed police arrived.

The officer in charge directed Sanchez to take cover behind a thick hedge. Suddenly Sanchez felt a heavy blow on his shoulder, which knocked him over. One of the drug dealers had thrown a heavy object out of a top floor window and Sanchez was in the wrong place even though he was behind some bushes. His participation in the raid was therefore short. A police officer approached and said, "I think you should go to hospital Sir, that seems a nasty blow." Sanchez demurred at first but the pain was intense so an ambulance was called.

He was not happy about going to hospital but realised the sense of it when he was told that a bone in his shoulder was very heavily bruised: he was lucky not to have sustained a broken shoulder. It was extremely painful and the doctor gave him some painkillers and said, "I advise you not to drive your car until that gets much easier". Later Sanchez realised he could easily have been shot; the hedge would not have protected him from a bullet, however, two more villains had joined the other three waiting to be processed. Many drugs were found in the third raid but, unfortunately, no one was caught.

The two men and one woman from the first raid were interrogated and it was found that the woman had little to do with the business; she was handed back to the local police for any action. Of the two men, one was obviously the boss and the EUDforce people concentrated on him.

Like all the people brought in he was reluctant to give any information about how he obtained his supplies. He said that he would at least be alive in prison; he was sure that talking would cause him to be killed or at best beaten up. Sanchez told him that he would arrange for a new identity if he gave information that was valuable. This interested the man and he was given time to think about it. His companion was questioned heavily but it became obvious that he knew nothing important. He was just a hired man. Again, the local police took care of him.

EUDforce men questioned the first man who had been given time to think about his decision. The questioner said, "I am not going to give you any more time. You have two choices," he warned, "You must tell me what I want to know or it is thirty years in our prison. This prison is not a nice place to be, no televisions and comfort I can assure you."

The man had clearly thought deeply before being questioned again: he decided to talk after all, although he still kept muttering about being killed. Sanchez noted the common thread about being killed. He asked the police whether many murders did take place in the event of information being given. They did not have any statistics on this but knew of a few cases where it was likely that information given could have been the reason.

When the man talked he said, "My supplier is somewhere in Harwich but I do not know the place where he lives. He drops off a regular supply of stuff for me, mostly heroin and cocaine, and tells me the drop-off place by phone the night before." Sanchez discussed the information with his staff and they decided that the method of supply could probably enable them to organise a backtracking exercise to find the supplier's place of residence. It would all depend on getting the correct information from their detainee. The man agreed to cooperate fully and he was released, under the supervision of two of Sanchez's men. He knew that any failure to cooperate would result in immediate imprisonment. As a further precaution, the man was shadowed in case he slipped away from his guardians and did a runner.

All did not go to plan and despite careful tracking most of the way the trackers lost their quarry a mile or so before the centre of Harwich. Somehow or other the man managed to fool them just as they were close. They were sure he did not know that they were following. He was just careful. At last, after two more attempts, the supplier was tracked, and caught. This was higher up the chain than they had achieved before. The man was brought back and held safely for questioning, in London.

From the second raid where Sanchez was hurt, the two men already faced a considerable time in prison because of the firearms offences. However, Sanchez wanted to find out more about the drugs. Once again, it appeared that one of the two was the leader and the questioner assured the man that he would get some protection if his information was worthwhile.

As they were hopeful that he would talk eventually, the questioners were more patient than normal. After a day and a night he decided to tell what he knew. The information was most interesting. He had drop-offs of drugs, but no warning of the exact date, merely a fairly regular timing. The EUDforce decided this time to mount an operation to catch the supplier when he delivered the drugs. By surveying over a long period, they hoped to encompass the delivery date and, after being given the usual two choices, the man agreed to take part in the operation to catch his supplier.

The plan went well until the main supplier was believed to be close to delivering the drugs. An over-enthusiastic young police constable blundered upon the detectives waiting and started to question the reasons for their presence. The action nearly gave the game away until a senior detective managed to convince the constable that all was well and they were in the middle of a tricky job. Complete with his load of drugs, the main supplier was caught and shipped for questioning to the EUDforce station.

There were now two main suppliers in Sanchez's jail. This was the highest level of supplier yet. After initial questioning without the usual threats, the Harwich man said he would cooperate if a firm agreement to help him could be arranged. Sanchez agreed with the proviso that the information was good; and this time he meant it, as the information could be valuable. He arranged for two of his more experienced men to continue to talk to the person who was now called 'the Harwich man'.

The Harwich man gave more details of his sources. It appeared that one of the boats that plied regularly between the Hook of Holland and Harwich brought in considerable quantities of illegal drugs. The questioners asked, "Do you know how the drugs get to Holland?"

"No, I have no idea at all. I only know my immediate source." The questioners were inclined to believe him but a further question remained.

"What is the name of the boat?"

The Harwich man replied, "It may seem funny but I have never seen the full name. It is something like 'Sea P…' but I don't know exactly. I get the stuff from a man on the Quay."

After consulting Sanchez it was decided that a full scale raid would take place on the boat when it next berthed in Harwich. One of Sanchez's men was sent to consult shipping information to see the next dockings. A police unit with dogs, customs officers and some of Sanchez's men would all be present. All information was passed to the intelligence team. They now must wait until the boat was due. More questioning of the Harwich man also revealed a number of people that he supplied. This was very useful and the police had a field day arresting another twenty-five drug suppliers and their customers.

The other supplier in the EUDforce jail was very nervous about giving information but admitted he was equally scared of thirty years in jail. After several lots of questioning and with the thirty years prevalent in his mind the man finally cracked. He said, "The drugs come from a boat berthed in a small seaside town in Sussex, called Rusthampton. The name of the boat is Zanadu, a schooner, usually berthed by a walkway on the other side of the river to the Yacht club."

Sanchez decided to go on this trip himself together with two of his staff. He called in at a larger port along the coast and saw the customs people who agreed to send one of their members with the EUDforce team. The boat was a two masted schooner, as the supplier had said, some twenty metres in length and capable of ocean travel.

The customs man, who was allowed by Sanchez, to board first, called out, "Anyone around, Customs here." A few moments passed and then a man of medium height, slim build and a ruddy complexion came out to see them.

"Hi, what can I do for you?"

The customs man answered, "We are having a general check on all ocean class boats, nothing specific, just like to have a look round. Is that ok?"

The owner of the boat looked worried but raised no objections and replied, "Sure, if you must, but I have not had this sort of check before."

"Oh, it's just a bit of routine work Sir; you know we get these jobs occasionally."

Sanchez could see that the customs man knew what he was doing as he searched the boat with a thoroughness that Sanchez admired. Not long after he started the customs man phoned the local police, explained who he was and requested a drug-finding dog to be brought to the boat. Ten minutes later the dog and handler arrived; they started another search and the dog soon found two hiding places and a large haul of drugs. The customs officer had suspected that the drugs were there but needed confirmation by the dog. Sanchez told the man he was going to be arrested and taken to London. The boat owner said, "I want to call a lawyer."

Although Sanchez did not intend to allow this, he said that it might be possible, but only in London. The boat owner was not happy, but he was soon put in a police car and they all set off back to the London EUDforce station. Sanchez left the customs man to attend to the impounding of the boat and the retention of the drugs as evidence later. A long series of questioning then took place in London with the boat owner but he was a very hard man to break.

The thirty-year threat did not seem to move him and Sanchez was disappointed at the lack of progress. There must be a weakness he could exploit; he wondered if the man really believed the prison threat. He decided to go for broke and told two of his men to take the drug supplier away to Belgium. He thought that time in the prison where the regime was deliberately tough might alter the man's mind.

Now his next chance of a breakthrough was the arrival of the ship, the 'Sea P…'. He had received information from his men was that it was likely to be the 'Sea Princess', no other ship was found that was 'Sea P….' Sanchez asked himself whether this ship would bring them nearer to the top of the chain of drug suppliers. The whole business was like standing on a moving stage trying to catch a moving target. He would feel more frustrated as the job went on; drug barons were not easily caught.

10

The moneylender was a man of many parts; he had contacts both in Afghanistan and in the West. In his younger days, part of his activities took him to Europe on several occasions. Despite his youthful appearance, he had been in this business for a long time and he knew a lot about the criminal fraternity. Simple money lending was not the only work he did; he provided finance for projects where the returns were good even though they might be illegal. He was also engaged in money laundering on a large scale. Many criminals had reason to curse the moneylender for the high rewards he wanted for his help. However, they knew that without that help their illicit rewards might be worthless.

There had been several attempts on his life but he still lived to continue his work. In his original dealings with Omar Rahim he had put up the money for the enterprise. Whether enterprise is a good word for the things that Omar did is somewhat doubtful, of course. The moneylender arranged for the proceeds to be banked for Omar, in a Western bank, but he never told Omar how he did it. He provided a system for Omar, and as long as this was followed the money went into the correct account. Omar never thought that anything could harm these arrangements.

The moneylender creamed some money off this to cover his repayments on the original loan plus interest that helped to build up his own considerable wealth. One of his more profitable ventures was taking in money, at a premium of course, from people who had suddenly come into money from some illegal transaction. He then provided them with Afghanis from honest sources; the clients were usually satisfied because otherwise they could not use the original money. What he did with this money nobody knows but it went somewhere to his advantage.

Undoubtedly, the moneylender sailed very close to the wind and the police were certainly suspicious of him. It was one thing to be suspicious of the moneylender but direct evidence was never forthcoming. He had no illusions about what could happen to him with the sort of people he dealt with; they would not tolerate any double-crossing on his part. There was always the more subtle danger of some criminal being so dissatisfied that the police might receive an anonymous letter that would trap the moneylender.

Nevertheless, life went on and the moneylender prospered.

While he was visiting another town in Afghanistan where he was due to pay an unpleasant individual a quantity of Afghanis for services rendered, he nearly met his fate. The man thought the amount was not enough and threatened the moneylender with a knife. The moneylender was cut badly, but managed to get away in the ensuing struggle.

In the course of his activities, he was visiting another town some two hundred kilometres from home and he was musing about his life. He sat in the hotel lounge and he wondered how much longer he would pursue the more dangerous types of work. He could go to the West or live a quiet life in Meyhabul, a town that he quite liked. He thought more about this as he walked down to dinner, he knew by the law of averages the police might catch up with him. He decided there and then that he would see to this job and one other that was already arranged.

It was late that night that he met the man he was going to deal with, a man he distrusted. The man always wanted a larger share than had been arranged and the moneylender wondered how the meeting would go tonight. As usual, the man wanted more and the moneylender was not in the mood to give in, this was a deal where he would stick to the original figures.

Two things happened that night that further strengthened his resolve to finish the dangerous parts of his job. He knew it would be a wrench to do this as they provided a large part of his income. The first was the anticipated unpleasant meeting he had with the man; it took far too long and he was tired of these protracted negotiations. The second was the sudden appearance of the police who must have been tipped off about the meeting.

How they knew about it was a lasting mystery to the moneylender but his mind was now firmly fixed – only one more job of this sort then he would retire to a quieter life. He was lucky not to be caught this night and only by hiding in a very unpleasant shed, which had previously housed goats did he escape detection. The smell was dreadful and he wondered how he was to get back into the hotel without the smell being obvious to everyone. It was nearly two hours later when he dared to emerge hoping the police had gone; he heard nothing as he emerged from the shed.

Fortunately, there was no one about when he went back into the hotel; he showered very thoroughly to remove the smell and went to bed. What happened to the other man the moneylender never found out; he assumed he too had escaped. He arrived home in Meyhabul some days later, tired but thankful he had made a decision about his future. He could now live a more peaceful life after the next and last job.

It was a few weeks later that the moneylender set off on the job which was to be the last one. It was dangerous for two reasons. He had to take a large quantity of Afghanis for people who would just as soon rob him as adhere to the arrangements already made. The second reason was the possibility that the police might get wind of the operation. Other people might not be as careful as he was. He was due this time to accept a large quantity of jewels for the money he carried, so he was acting as a fence but already had a customer for the jewels.

He did not deal in stolen jewellery very often but he knew these jewels; they were Russian and were of considerable value. The robbers had stolen them, with others, from a wealthy family but the moneylender was sure they did not realise their true worth. The project therefore was attractive and he should make a considerable profit.

The meeting was some distance from Meyhabul, one hundred and sixty kilometres south from his home. It was not an easy journey, he would have to change buses three times, stay in two hotels for two nights and he was wary about being robbed. He always kept a small Smith and Wesson M&P9, 9 mm pistol on his person; he had used it once before to protect himself and he would not hesitate to use it again.

There were some passengers on the bus that he wondered about, they looked as though they might cheerfully cut someone's throat; he remained on guard. This, he thought, was another good reason for stopping this kind of work. The journeys were invariably long and he felt more tired than he used to do. He finally reached his destination and made acquaintance with the robbers who showed him the jewels.

They were just as he had been informed; he would make a considerable amount of money from this deal.

Before he met the men he carefully hid his Afghanis, he did not want them to be taken from him, before he acquired the jewels. There was some bargaining about the price the men wanted but finally a deal was struck and the moneylender arranged for the exchange to take place quietly in the public part of the eating-house. As soon as this was done, the moneylender slipped away to the bus station. He watched carefully to make sure he was not followed.

On arrival he went into the very basic toilet and strapped the jewel pouch to his chest with a long bandage he had brought with him. He felt a little more secure after doing this and looked around to see if there was a timetable to tell him when he might catch a bus. He could not find any such help but another individual was waiting so the moneylender asked him, "Do you happen to know when the next bus is due?"

The man replied, "I believe one should be along in about two hours' time but you know how badly they run."

"Thanks, yes I do know what you mean. When I came it was pretty late." The moneylender moved to another part of the bus station, sat down on the rickety seat, pulled his coat around him and prepared for a long, quiet wait.

He had waited for about an hour when he thought he noticed two figures moving nearer to him. By this time, it was getting dusk and he was not sure what he had seen. However, it was not long before his fears were realised; he recognised one of the men approaching. He made preparations to protect himself as he knew what was going to happen: the robbers were going to try to get the jewels back. He slowly drew the pistol from his pocket, kept it out of sight beneath his coat and waited.

The man approached with a knife drawn and demanded the return of the jewels. As he neared, he waved the knife at the moneylender. The moneylender backed away. He did not want to shoot the man if he could avoid it. On one hand, it would be heard a long way away on this quiet evening, and on the other hand, the police might be around. There was no escape if he waited much longer.

As the man approached again, threatening him with the knife, he drew the gun hoping the sight of it might deter the man from continuing. Unfortunately, the attacker seemed to be more determined than ever and rushed at the moneylender.

The gun fired before the moneylender realised he had pulled the trigger and the man fell down before him. The noise seemed deafening. As the man fell down the moneylender slipped into the shadows, wiped the gun clean and hid it beneath some old wood rubbish. He then ran back to where the man lay and shouted for help; several people came to see what the noise was about and the moneylender told them he had heard a shot and came to see what had happened.

A few minutes later the police arrived and questioned all the people who had arrived after the shot. When the police asked the moneylender, he could say honestly that he thought he had seen two figures earlier and supposed that one of the two must have done the shooting. After some time the police retired from the scene, murder was not unusual and the moneylender's suggestion of the two men seemed to satisfy them. They searched for a long time after that and were still at it when the bus arrived.

It was another long and weary journey before he arrived home at last; he slept until lunchtime the next day and started thinking about the last part of this job: the sale of the jewels. The buyer lived about twenty-five kilometres from Meyhabul so the moneylender decided to go in his car this time; he knew the road and he certainly did not fancy another uncomfortable bus ride.

He arrived at his destination in the late morning and rang the bell at a large ranch style house. It was not long before a servant opened the door and enquired the name of the caller. Having explained who he was, the moneylender was invited into a large comfortable library where he sat down to wait until the owner of the house came into the room.

"Good morning, nice to see you again, are you keeping well?" he said as he offered his hand to the moneylender. The moneylender smiled and acknowledged the greeting as he grasped the owner's hand and replied that he was quite well. As they shook hands, the owner said, "Let us go into the other room, the chairs are more comfortable and we can have coffee." The servant brought in coffee and biscuits and they talked about generalities for twenty minutes or so before the owner said, "So, we had better look at the jewels."

The moneylender produced the pouch of the jewels and spread then on the table. "Beautiful, beautiful," said the buyer as he examined the jewels under a magnifying glass, "Yes my friend, these are the ones I want, they really are perfect."

After a small amount of discussion about the price they agreed a figure and the moneylender was handed a large amount of Afghanis; he was very satisfied. "If you have any more liked these I would be interested," said the owner and the moneylender smiled but said nothing; he had done his last job. After more small talk, the moneylender took his leave and departed. His first job was to bank the money in Meyhabul – as he had done many times. He breathed a sigh of relief after this and thought, now he could relax, he had done his last illegal job. He was not aware that this action might change his life.

11

Sanchez now had two slices of unfinished business; the wait for the Sea Princess from Holland and the yacht owner who did not want to talk. He did wonder whether putting the boat owner in prison quickly had been the correct decision but it was done now. There was another large problem. Sanchez knew he must get other stations open very soon, otherwise only a small section of the drugs business could be targeted. He rang the Minister who was getting suitable premises for him, "Good morning Minister, Sanchez here, how are the sites going, will there be any ready very soon?"

The Minister told him, "Will you wait just a minute while I check up with my people but I think some are almost ready." He came back almost immediately. "Pedro, in three days there will be seven sites ready enough for you to get started. The sites are at Birmingham, Nottingham, Carlisle, York, Plymouth, Exeter and Swansea. I think I can promise that it will not be long before more will be available. I will keep you posted"

Sanchez thanked the Minister and put the phone down. The information was better than he expected. Staffing was now his top priority. He had to get more staff to work under the existing head people. He chose fourteen of his staff to get ready to take up their posts as first and second in command of each site. All his senior people had been well taught by him, at every opportunity, and had experience of procedure at the London EUDforce station. He knew also that the backing staff would have to follow quickly. He emailed Talbot to report this progress.

He arranged to see the Commissioner again in order to talk to him about more support staff. After consultation with the EU and the British Government, Talbot suggested that Sanchez should always talk to the Commissioner rather than individual Chief Constables. After the usual pleasantries Sanchez said, "I'm looking this time for any Inspectors, sergeants and other ranks particularly those in drugs units. The number is likely to be a total of three hundred sixty men and women; the number needed immediately is eighty-four. However I think the rest will be wanted quite soon, as the accommodation availability is coming along well."

The Commissioner raised an eyebrow at these numbers but then answered, "It might take me a while to manage this number but as you will eventually take over the drug units I hope the Chief Constables will get the people you want fairly quickly." He thought privately that policing as he knew it was going in directions that he was not sure about. His instructions from the Government were clear: all assistance must be given to EUDforce.

Sanchez was awakened the next morning by his mobile phone alarm and almost immediately afterwards his phone rang. He picked it up and a voice said, "Sorry to ring you early Sir, but we now know that the Sea Princess is coming in tomorrow night at around nine p.m."

Sanchez replied, "Thanks for that, we shall have to get cracking now. See you in about half an hour." Arrangements had already been made for a team to assemble when the boat's arrival was known. Now all the relevant authorities had to be notified. Sanchez phoned the officer in charge at the London EUDforce station and told him to alert the people that would comprise the team to meet the ship.

The next day at eight p.m. the team assembled on the dockside, away from where the Sea Princess was due to arrive. Sanchez wanted to see if there were any dealers waiting for their drugs. By eight fifty-five there was no evidence of anything about, except some refrigerated Lorries which were waiting for the ship.

The drivers were escorted away by local police who examined their credentials and looked them up on the police database. They all appeared to be genuine drivers for their companies and were cleared but kept in custody until the Sea Princess had been dealt with. Sanchez decided that when the Sea Princess and her crew had been examined he would let the dogs check the waiting Lorries just in case.

There were two handlers with their dogs, three customs officers, and six members of EUDforce, together with a dozen police of varying ranks. Sanchez had received information on the Sea Princess and its owner, covering a period of over ten years. He was surprised to find that no problems or the slightest suspicion of any wrongdoing had ever been recorded. He would have expected something to be on record if drug running was an ongoing activity. Whatever had been going on had obviously been quietly successful.

Much earlier in the day, In Holland, the Sea Princess had been loaded with farm produce which went into a refrigerated hold and dry cargo in the other of the two main holds. Compared with the normal cargo ship the Sea Princess was really small. It had been constructed some two years before the present ownership more as an experiment in some construction ideas than for serious use. It was only thirty-three metres in length, a beam of ten and a half metres and two main holds. Notwithstanding its small size, it suited the owner, Captain Henry MacThomas very well. The quantity of the farm produce was usually fairly constant. However there was not much dry cargo this time and the Captain wondered how many more trips he could afford to make.

The Captain was a big man, a typical image of a seaman with a clipped beard, a full moustache and greying hair. He was proud of the Sea Princess but he was aware that a small cargo boat working with small loads was probably nearly at the end of a way of life. After the loading was complete the ship started off for its voyage to Harwich. It chugged its way at a steady ten knots; the weather was good and Henry did not expect any problems.

He travelled blissfully unaware of the unpleasant ending of his journey. Among other short trips, the Captain made this particular journey to Harwich about every six weeks. Eleven years ago he had met a Dutch exporter of farm produce and had been delivering his produce ever since. They had become good friends and the arrangement suited them both. He also collected a variety of dry cargo to fill his other hold and increase his profit.

He was disappointed that it was not so much this time. The operation was not a big money spinner as he had a small crew to pay as well as the normal ship expenses. He did make enough to save for his later years but there was no fortune in the work. He liked the life and had many friends in Holland and Harwich.

The Captain heard his engineer grumbling about the engines, "We have to get these valves replaced Henry, one day I'll not be able to move them, then they will be stuck and so will we."

"All right John we'll do it in Harwich, I know they want attention."

John, the ship's engineer had been with the Captain ever since he had started the business; he was much more a friend than an employee. There were four other employees, a first officer and three seamen.

After its uneventful voyage the Sea Princess pulled slowly into the allocated berth, all lines were secured and a gangplank put down. Although it was nine twenty p.m. there were plenty of lights illuminating the berth area. As the Captain walked down the gangplank he was surprised to see the welcoming party including the dogs. One of the crew had also seen the party on the quayside and tried to hide behind a stanchion near the side of the ship. Unfortunately, he approached too near the edge and slipped over the side into the water. A loud splash was easily heard as, not being able to swim, he struggled to keep afloat. One of Sanchez's men raced to the water's edge and saw the crewman struggling. He ran down some steps, dived in and rescued the man.

Sanchez approached the man coming down the gangplank and said, "You are the Captain?"

"Indeed I am, Henry MacThomas is the name; what is all this about?"

Sanchez said, "We have information that you are carrying drugs and we are going to search the vessel."

"Ridiculous rubbish," the Captain replied loudly, "There have never been any drugs on my ship, I hate the drugs trade."

"Well we have information that you do have drugs on your ship and we are going to search," repeated Sanchez. "Where are the rest of your crew?"

The Captain replied, "Apart from the one who apparently fell in the water the rest are on the deck, I assume they are still there."

Sanchez ordered three of the policemen to collect the crew and bring them back to the police van. One was already there, rather wet and frightened. The first to board the ship were the customs men and the two dog handlers with their dogs trained to find any drugs. They started to search the dry cargo hold first, as this seemed the most likely place, rather than in the farm produce. Their reasoning was that it was easier for anyone to slip drugs into this hold. It was not long before one of the customs men returned to tell Sanchez that a haul of drugs had been found in the dry cargo hold. Sanchez decided to leave most of the staff at the ship and return to London with the Captain and his crew.

They departed in the police van with two EUDforce men. He would have a lot more freedom to question them at the EUDforce station. He put the ship's crew, including the Captain, into separate cells and left them until the morning. Fortunately, he'd had his second set of cells temporarily installed. The prisoners were fed, given blankets and told they would be questioned in the morning. Sanchez thought that a night in the cells might loosen tongues. The Captain was very indignant about the whole affair and said he had never touched drugs in his life.

The next morning Sanchez arrived to question the crew. He started with the Captain, "You know why you are here Captain?" Henry MacThomas looked up at Sanchez and said,

"This is quite unbelievable, as I have already said I definitely have no idea how the drugs got into my ship. I have never knowingly carried any or would think of such a thing."

"But they were there, on your ship, yes?"

The Captain replied, "I know that because you found them but I have no idea at all how they got there. I have been doing this run for nearly eleven years and never had any problems before."

Sanchez asked, "What about your crew? How do you rate all of them?" The Captain looked up at Sanchez and said,

"Well, John, my engineer, has been with me for over ten years – my first officer five, no six now and the other crew members about three or four years."

Sanchez interjected, "But what do you know about them?"

"How do you know anybody?" countered the Captain, "They have always seemed ok and John, the engineer, is a good friend of mine." Sanchez ordered one of his men to escort the Captain back to his cell and with two of his staff started questioning the rest of the crew.

Prior to this, another member of his staff was ordered by Sanchez to talk to the Paris HQ and see if any information could be gleaned about the crew including the Captain.

After the questioning of the crew had started, one of Sanchez's men knocked on the interview door, opened it a little, and motioned to Sanchez that he should come out for a moment. "We have some important information about one of the crew: his name is Eric Stewart." Sanchez realised this was the crewman who jumped or fell into the water.

"What do you know?" asked Sanchez.

"Only that he has been cautioned before about taking drugs, he might be your man."

"He may have been trying to escape instead of falling in then?" Sanchez said.

The questioning continued in the same way as before and eventually Eric Stewart was brought before Sanchez and two of his staff. One of the questioners was a woman; previously a Chief Inspector in a drugs squad unit. Sanchez had found her to be a shrewd questioner and considered a superior position for her in the future. He also experienced some unusual feelings about this woman. She was very attractive and

Sanchez had not felt this way before. He had never taken much interest in women although he had been out with one or two. They had never appealed to him as this woman did.

It was late at night when, after very detailed grilling by several teams of the station Stewart finally decided to tell what he knew. "So where do you obtain the drugs?" asked one of the questioners.

"A man gives then to me at the quayside in Holland to have them loaded into the dry cargo hold. They are specially marked with black stripes so that I can find them when we land," Stewart answered.

"And how do you pay this man?"

"Its all cash on the spot, otherwise I would not get any stuff."

The questioner spoke again, "So you must have seen your supplier; what does he look like?"

Stewart thought for a moment, "He is ordinary looking, medium height, black hair I think and he usually wears a long black coat, like riders wear."

The questioners looked at each other. "Not much to go on," one commented. The questioning continued. "Where do you think this supplier gets his stuff from?"

"I am sorry but I have no idea at all, I just met him and that is that." Stewart added, "If it's any help, the Captain and other members of the crew would never know anything about this. I put everything in myself, I have been doing this for about six years."

Sanchez believed the part about the Captain and the rest of the crew and decided to release them. He phoned the Customs people to let the Captain have his ship back. There was no point in retaining it; he knew this was an unusual procedure but in his opinion, it served no purpose to do otherwise. What the questioners were anxious to find out was how they could trap the man who supplied Stewart. "When would you be getting your next load?" one of the questioners asked.

"I will have to look at my diary to see when it will be."

The EUDforce staff looked through Stewart's belongings and found the diary. Stewart thumbed through it and said,

"It should be in five weeks time, on the Friday. I think you will be able to check for certain the same as I do, from the shipping lists nearer the time."

Stewart was asked if he would cooperate in an operation to catch his supplier. This might, if all went well, help to minimize his prison sentence. He readily agreed and, having obtained the best information he could, Sanchez communicated the details to HQ in Paris. He suggested that they use Stewart to try to catch his supplier.

Talbot came back with a positive response, so Stewart was kept in the London site cells for just under five weeks, by which time, hopefully, he could be used as bait.

The plan looked very straightforward as many plans do; time would tell.

12

Sanchez now had twenty sites working and some very good results were being recorded. The Commissioner in Scotland Yard who had been privately worried about the whole EUDforce scheme was now quite enthusiastic. There was good co-operation between the Yard drugs unit and the EUDforce men. Sanchez, although fairly satisfied, had not achieved the real breakthrough that he wanted. While more and more suppliers at different levels were being unearthed the leads to the very big boys and growers were not being found by his teams. There was little doubt that the big boys were hurting as avenues of sales were being slowly closed; it was the personal satisfaction that Sanchez was missing but he realised this might not be available.

He thought about what else could be done although he knew that he could not simply reach out to drug producing countries and take any direct action. The main problem was that several of these countries like Mexico, Columbia, Afghanistan and Pakistan had great internal problems of their own and had little spare time for attending to requests from others. There was some cooperation of course but maybe it could be improved quite a lot thought Sanchez. The whole operation had been running for only eight weeks, was he expecting too much in that time?

The ship owner at Rusthampton was still in prison and had not shown any signs of giving information. He wondered, was his gamble of putting the man in prison a bad idea? Maybe he should have been more patient. He decided to go to the prison and have another go at questioning. He would take the woman police Inspector with him. Sanchez, normally a very self-confident individual did have self-doubts that he had not experienced before.

He also had two other matters on his mind.

One was to interview the remaining Chief Superintendents or Superintendents to make up the shortfall in his original quest. The other was personal: the growing attraction he felt for the woman Chief Inspector. His mother, when she was alive, used to tell him he would know when the right woman came along. He felt that he knew that time had arrived: this lady was different from the ones he had seen before. Perhaps his mother was right after all.

In the next two weeks, information came in that looked very positive. It came from the Birmingham site and was due to a main supplier of some forty other suppliers. After persuasion that was definitely not in the human rights legislation, he decided to tell what he knew. He claimed that not only did he know about his own supplier but also about the people who had supplied him, who were the importers and would certainly know the next link in the chain.

Sanchez left his staff to get on with their work and thought more about the whole set up. The original terms of reference by the EU Committee stated that he had to find a successor to manage the entire EU drugs business. Clearly, this was not possible and was ridiculous; the only way was a head in each country. He could then coordinate these heads. Continuing with this thought, he looked through the records of the higher echelons of the people he had.

One man stood out as a possible contender. He then thought of the woman Chief Inspector but decided that although she was very good, the top job in the UK was not for her at this time. Sanchez spoke to Maurice Talbot via video phone and discussed with him all his thoughts about the job. "What do you think, Maurice?"

Talbot replied, "You must have read my mind Pedro, I absolutely agree with what you have said. I see no difficulty with the Committee. It was their first general idea at the time but it is clearly impossible to just have one man in charge, as they suggested."

Sanchez then turned to the subject of Eric Stewart, from the Sea Princess, who he was holding in his cells. He suggested to Talbot that he send Eric Stewart to him, so that all was ready to intercept the supplier that Stewart had identified.

The man Sanchez had picked to be the head of the UK operation was presently in charge of the York station. Sanchez therefore travelled there with his replacement, and to tell Chief Superintendent Roger Taylor that he had been selected to head the EUDforce in the UK. This appointment was for the drugs war and if the job was to entail more types of crime then a reassessment might be called for. Sanchez assured Taylor that he hoped that any change would not occur and that he would remain in that position. Taylor and Sanchez returned to London, which would be the headquarters of the EUDforce.

The Birmingham information turned out to be valuable; they captured the Importer and were working on him. He was a much tougher individual than the man who had given him away. He was Asian and was quite adamant that he would say nothing. Sanchez was informed of these developments and, accompanied by the woman Chief Inspector, went to

Birmingham. They wanted to see for themselves what sort of individual they were up against.

Travelling with the woman by train, Sanchez learned that her name was Rebecca and that she had always wanted to be in the Police service. There was little doubt that Pedro Sanchez was 'smitten' and it showed in his behaviour. Sanchez knew he was falling in love and fervently hoped that she felt the same about him. Unfortunately, there was not much time to know her better for the time being: they were all too busy. Whatever the protocols in this situation he was still to find out; two police, one an employee and the other her boss might be frowned upon.

They arrived to find no change in the situation; the man refused to say anything. Sanchez decided to adopt the hard man and soft woman approach to see if they could tease any information out. They had the man brought into the interview room and Sanchez saw in front of him an obviously frightened man. "What are you frightened of?" Sanchez asked.

The man then adopted a somewhat truculent attitude and said, "I'm not frightened, you don't scare me."

Sanchez asked, "How would you like thirty years in a hard Labour prison?"

"It does not worry me. At least I would be alive," replied the man.

"So you are frightened of someone trying to kill you?" The man looked straight in front and said nothing but his demeanour said everything.

Rebecca intervened, "We understand the position, we have seen it all before." She went on, "What if we gave you a new identity so that you could never be recognised again."

The man looked at her with a small amount of interest and said, "I don't believe it can be done as easily as that, someone will find out."

"Indeed it can be done, I can promise you that you would have a completely different name, a job and if you have a wife or partner we can do the same for her. Do you have any children?"

"No, not at the moment."

"Well, what about it?" asked Rebecca? "We will do our part if you agree but the information must be true and worthwhile."

The man said, "I am not sure about all this, it sounds too good to be true. Why should I trust you?" Sanchez interjected,

"You will have to weigh that up against thirty years in a very uncomfortable prison."

The man said, "Can I think about it, please?"

Rebecca agreed to the request, "Of course, we'll give you a few minutes." Sanchez and Rebecca retired from the interview room and went back to their office.

"What do you think Rebecca?" asked Sanchez.

"I think he will talk, how much value I don't know," They busied themselves for five minutes and then went back to their interview. When they started talking to the man again he seemed to be on the verge of not talking after all. Rebecca wondered if their efforts were going to pay off but after some more light persuasion she managed to get the man to tell her what he knew. He said,

"I trust the lady and I'll tell you what you want to know."

"What can you tell us then?" enquired Sanchez.

"I get my stuff from a ship called the 'Eastern Gem' which comes from Pakistan. I have to pay on delivery in dollars."

"How do you know when to start looking for its arrival date," asked Sanchez. He added, "Or is it very regular?"

The man thought for a moment then said, "It makes the trip roughly every two months so I start looking in the shipping lists about a week before."

"Is it always the same person you speak to?" Rebecca asked.

"Yes," he said, "it has been the same person for the last three years or so."

"If we help you in the way we have proposed, we shall want you to meet the ship and your contact again as normal. There must be no action on your part to make the contact suspicious"

"Yes, I understand, but I want your people near when it happens. I shall not feel safe if they are not."

Rebecca assured the man that to make sure there was no problem he would be surrounded by police,

That afternoon, several more reports came into the London office one of which seemed to offer hope of an important result. An informer had told another office that a very large consignment of drugs was on its way to Felixstowe and would arrive tomorrow morning. Sanchez swung into action and arranged for a welcoming party.

The ship was searched and customs' dogs discovered drugs, but the aftermath was not pleasant. On board, as well as the drugs, were two illegal immigrants. These were not of the usual type; these men had guns and used them. One of Sanchez's men was shot dead and a customs man seriously injured. There were also two policemen injured. It was not until an armed response team arrived that the situation came under control.

Sanchez was sad about the man who was killed and the others who were injured. What made it worse for Sanchez was that one of the injured policemen was the commissioner's nephew. Sanchez phoned the Commissioner to tell him how sorry he was about the nephew and hoped the recovery would be swift. He also had another duty to carry out; a letter of sympathy to the relatives of the dead EUDforce man.

After an exciting but somewhat sad day, Sanchez decided to ask Rebecca out to dinner. She accepted willingly and Sanchez was really looking forward to this, as he had not relaxed for many weeks.

He was also thinking about the next moves in the drugs business. There were two more good chances now; first was Eric Stewart in Holland, the other was the ship from Pakistan. After some time the thought of Rebecca seemed much more important and he concentrated on dressing carefully for dinner.

The dinner was the first time they had relaxed together and they enjoyed the feeling. Rebecca was quite aware of how Sanchez felt; she felt the same for him but in her position thought it better to go a bit slow. After dinner, they walked down by the river and Sanchez was captivated by his companion. It was not long before he held her hand and they had several kisses on the way. Sanchez confessed his feelings for her and she acknowledged that she felt the same for him. He took her back to her hotel and went to bed feeling quite optimistic about life in general.

Life however was not always predictable as Sanchez would find out in the weeks to come. The people who were at the top of the distribution of illegal drugs were still practically undented by the efforts of the EUDforce. There was still a huge amount of work to do.

13

Omar Rahim was now in a poor state of health and despite repeated requests from Ahmed and Hamid he was loath to pursue the subject. There was no doubt something had to be done but it seemed he could not summon up the courage to get on with it. He urgently needed to get to a Western hospital to be further examined with more modern equipment. If the original diagnosis was confirmed then he could have the operation where the success rate would be higher.

Finally one day when he found himself out of breath after about fifteen yards of walking he went to Ahmed and said, "All right Ahmed, make the arrangements."

"I think you are wise Sir, you could get so bad that you could not travel. You know that Hamid can do everything for you, he has turned out to be a remarkable young man."

"I know Ahmed, he is quite competent to run the whole place. I can leave him in charge and not worry about it"

Ahmed had already spent a lot of time on the internet researching the hospital where Omar had the best chance of a full recovery. He thought at first that the USA would be the best but Omar was not sure of his reception. He wondered whether anything might be known about him. He felt that he might get trapped there as the USA was hot on drugs. He had no real reason for his suspicion, but felt safer going to Europe.

They settled on the Royal Sussex Hospital in Brighton, Sussex, UK. Results were very good, over ninety-five percent as far as he could ascertain.

Ahmed made all the arrangements and booked the Grand Hotel on the seafront at Brighton. They could stay there as long as they needed to remain for the operation and the time Omar needed to recuperate before returning to Afghanistan.

Ahmed, who spoke good English, arranged for a private nurse and a doctor to be available after the operation. They had an uneventful journey from Meyhabul to Kabul and a long plane journey to Heathrow. The taxi brought them in comfort to the Grand where they settled into the suite of rooms pre-booked by Ahmed. Two days later Omar saw the consultant who would perform the operation. Omar spent a whole day undergoing a variety of tests and returned to the hotel very tired.

It was another two days later when he saw the consultant again. He told Omar about the results of his tests. He said, "Mr. Rahim, I have to say that you have left things a bit late and there is a greater risk as your tests revealed some weaknesses in your heart itself. The consultant continued, "However I think we can perform the operation and we will take every care of your heart. At least we are forewarned; you may need a pacemaker afterwards."

Omar was more worried than he had been before but knew that the only chance of a better life was to go ahead with the operation. Five days after that meeting Omar attended the hospital with Ahmed for the operation. The operation was difficult but successful and as the consultant had predicted a pacemaker was fitted. It took ten days in total including the time in the high dependency unit and a private ward for three days. Ahmed had been in every day to see his master and was pleased that all had gone well.

Once Omar was discharged, he and Ahmed spent their time walking gently on the front near their hotel; Omar felt better than he had done for a long time. Ahmed arranged for their flights home in a week from then.

Two days before they were due to travel to Heathrow Omar complained of a sick feeling and a pain in his stomach. The doctor was called and suspected appendicitis. Omar was sent back to hospital for further tests and an operation was performed. Omar survived the operation and they went back to the hotel for further recuperation: Ahmed had to cancel the flights. It was on the third day after this that Omar again felt unwell. The doctor was called immediately and said he thought complications had set in from the last operation.

Arrangements were made to go back in to hospital but within an hour, Omar was dead. Ahmed was in great confusion at this sudden change of events. He blessed the day that he had learned English, as without this knowledge he would have found things very difficult. He made all the arrangements for the funeral and cabled to Omar's bank for funds to be released to him for the funeral, hotel and hospital expenses.

It was fortunate to be in the UK as obtaining sterling funds was not difficult since the funds were lodged in dollars in the EU. Fortunately Ahmed had always had access to the bank account as he dealt with all the payments from the estate. However, when in Afghanistan, he arranged to access the funds through contacts that the moneylender had set up with Omar many years ago.

Ahmed was tempted, a little, to stay in Brighton as he quite liked the area; then he thought of Hamid and felt ashamed to leave him there on his own. He decided to return to Afghanistan to the estate to tell Hamid all that had occurred.

Hamid was very sad and felt a great responsibility.

After Ahmed had settled in, he called Hamid into his office. "Hamid, we have to look at Omar's will. I do not know what is in it but we must see what his wishes were."

Hamid looked up from a contemplative mood and replied, "Yes, yes, of course, I really don't know what we are going to do."

"Well let's see if the will can help us," answered Ahmed.

Ahmed carefully opened the document and pulled out a single sheet of paper. It was very simple and comprised two main statements and a paragraph under. Firstly, it made clear that the whole estate, everything including Omar's savings, amounting to five million dollars was to go to Hamid.

Secondly, the sum of one million dollars was for Ahmed.

The paragraph under these bequests simply wished that Ahmed would stay with Hamid until Hamid wished to leave.

Both men sat over a glass of wine and pondered on their situation. Ahmed knew he could retire now if he wished but the paragraph was on his mind. In any case, he thought, what would I do? Ahmed looked up to see Hamid watching him. Hamid was in a complete daze; the money and the responsibility were enormous. "What is it Hamid?" Ahmed queried.

"I was just thinking of the whole thing, are you going to retire now?" Ahmed and Hamid had got on very well together since Omar had been so unwell. In fact Ahmed, never having any children himself, was very fond of Hamid and treated him in an almost fatherly manner. He answered Hamid after thinking about the question for a minute or so.

"No, Hamid, I cannot see me retiring to some place where I would probably be bored stiff after a week or so." He continued, "We have a good life here, I like my job and I think you like yours so I think we'll stay."

Hamid was extremely pleased with Ahmed's answer and went to bed that night with very mixed feeling. On the one hand he was very sad that his uncle had died, on the other he was glad that Ahmed had decided to stay. Then a third feeling came over him; the total responsibility for the job he had to do and the enormous wealth he now apparently possessed.

He then thought of his wife, he had not seen her for a long time, would she come if he sent for her?

In the morning, Hamid felt calmer; there was work to do and he had to do it. There was no uncle to advise him, it was all up to him. He asked Ahmed to write to his wife. "I'm not very good at writing Ahmed; perhaps you could do it for me?"

Ahmed readily agreed and the letter was sent that day. The post was not very good so Hamid did not expect a reply for two weeks or more.

Hamid carried out all the tasks his Uncle had taught him and life settled in as before. Hamid could not really believe that this huge estate belonged to him; it was all a dream. He did not feel that he owned it; he was managing it for his uncle.

He confessed his thoughts to Ahmed who said, "My boy, it is yours. I understand how you feel, but your Uncle wanted you to have it, he wrote it down. You will feel different as time goes by."

"I suppose so," concurred Hamid, "But it is a very strange feeling, my Uncle had a very strong influence on me."

Other influences far away were going to make their presence felt in due course but again Hamid knew nothing about it.

In a village in Pakistan, life went on too, but not like the luxury in the estate of Hamid. This was the village where Mohammed, once the foreman of Omar Rahim, now lived. The villagers had taken him as one of their own after he had arrived half-dead from his long trek to Pakistan. Now he had a job for a few hours a week and contributed to the finances of the family where he lived. There was no television in the house nor could they afford a newspaper even if one was available. Their news from the world outside came via an old radio set.

Mohammed could neither read nor write but he liked to listen to the news. He had picked up some of the language and could understand a little. The only problem was the battery usage; these did not last very long. They were expensive so the family listened twice a day to the main news program.

One day while they were listening Mohammed just caught a mention of the EU forming a new police force to operate against the illegal drugs trade. He had tried to forget the terrible time he had endured at Rahim's estate: now at this mention it all came back with a rush.

He felt sick to think of all the cruelty the workers had to suffer, both physically and mentally at the hands of Omar Rahim. The thought began to smoulder in his mind: how could he get revenge.

Among the family was a young boy aged about twelve who could read and write. Mohammed began to think of a plan and asked the youngster whether he would write a letter for him. The young lad quickly agreed and Mohammed had now to formulate the details. He was determined to give as much information as possible. He had spoken to the pilot many times and knew where Omar took the heroin to meet the mule trains.

The young lad religiously wrote all that Mohammed told him and now Mohammed's final task was to think of an address for the letter. He decided to send it to the King of the UK as he had heard of him and did not know of anyone else. So Mohammed's letter found its way to an equerry of the King who promptly sent it to the Government. The Minister who received it was wise enough to get the letter interpreted by a Pakistan speaking person who told him that it contained details of a large drug production place in Afghanistan.

Luckily, this man knew of the EUDforce and passed the letter to Scotland Yard who gave it to Sanchez. He was delighted to receive it and immediately told Talbot about the contents.

Talbot decided that this was a job for the EU Foreign Office and gave them all the details. Unfortunately, Hamid Rahim knew nothing of the impending storm that might arise from this information.

14

Sanchez was waiting for any result from the meeting of Eric Stewart with the man who supplied his drugs. Waiting was a hard process for Sanchez; he liked much more activity.

It had been arranged that the Paris HQ would supervise the meeting so that the man could be caught with the money from Stewart. He would then be sent to London for questioning. Today was the day that Stewart had said the meeting was due.   Sanchez was hoping against hope that he would at last get nearer to the growers and main men behind the supplies. He realised that work was proceeding in the intelligence section, which up to now had achieved good successes. At least ten major suppliers high in the supply chain had been put out of business and large quantities of illegal drugs seized and destroyed.

It was not only that these suppliers were finished but whole networks of minor suppliers were also caught. They were all given the usual warning: get caught again and off to prison in Belgium. Statistics being generated showed that only one in one hundred of the people caught, re-offended.

Sanchez also remembered that the EU Foreign Office might come up with a good result from the Afghanistan letter by Mohammed the previous foreman on Omar's estate.

On the night of the meeting Stewart had been warned to adhere strictly to his instructions otherwise, it was a long prison sentence for him in Belgium. At the appointed time Stewart approached the man waiting on an unlit part of the quayside. "Stewart here, is that Hussein?"

"Yes, it is Hussein," he answered then said, "Have you brought the money."

"Yes, I have the usual amount. Have you got my stuff?"

"Yes, but not the usual amount, the price has gone up."

"How much?" asked Stewart.

"You will be able to buy three quarters of the previous amount for the same money."

Stewart said, "That seems one hell of a large increase in price. Are you sure about this?"

Hussein shrugged his shoulders but said nothing. Stewart tried to bargain as he would have been expected to do but the supplier was adamant: he was not interested in any bargaining process. Stewart examined the drugs contained in plastic bags in a large canvas bag, tasted a few samples and handed over the money. While this transaction was going on about a dozen men were circling, ready to make the last dash across the lighted part of the quay to the unlit portion where Stewart was collecting the bag of drugs.

Finally they did so, encircling the man: he gave up quietly. His options were very few with twelve men around him.

While Sanchez was working in his office in the London HQ, Taylor, now the head of the UK operations came to see him. "Pedro, you will remember the boat owner from Rusthampton, well he wishes to talk. I don't think he likes his life in Belgium."

"That is great news Roger, replied Sanchez, then added, "Get him over here as soon as you can. We must find out what ship contacts him with the drugs." Sanchez was pleased with this news and looked forward to interrogating the boat owner.

His phone rang about ten minutes after Taylor had been in to see him; this time it was Maurice Talbot. "Thought I would give you a ring myself Pedro, the news is good. We've got the man and he is on the way to you. His name is Hussein and I am also returning Stewart to you for any further action you will want to carry out."

Hussein arrived under guard the next day and the boat owner was expected in two days time from Belgium. Taylor and Rebecca questioned Hussein to see if somehow they could find out the source of his supplies.

"Who gives you the drugs from the ship?"

"I do not know his name but he is a ship's officer of some sort."

"Does he wear a uniform then?"

"Yes, I think he has two bars on his shoulders. I am not absolutely sure." The questioning went on,

"Is there anything else that you can remember about the man; what about the colour of this uniform?"

"I think it is a fawn colour."

"Anything else?" asked Rebecca.

"No, I can't think of anything, oh yes, he does wear a very large wristwatch. That's all I am afraid."

Rebecca carefully noted all this and gave the information to the intelligence section to see if they could find out more and Hussein was locked away until required later.

The boat owner arrived the next day and Sanchez joined Taylor and the head of the London EUDforce station to commence the interview. The boat owner confessed that prison had taught him a lesson: he would rather talk than stop there anymore. Sanchez thought to himself that the Belgium idea seemed to be working well enough.

Sanchez also brought in Rebecca as she undoubtedly obtained more from prisoners. He left the questioning to the others and preferred to listen as he wanted very much to savour the moment.

"Where do you get your supplies?" asked Taylor.

"I meet a ship in mid channel and they are passed over very quickly."

"What ship is it?"

"It's called the 'Rainbow' and comes from Mexico. Of course it will be on its way back by now."

Rebecca asked, "When is it due again?"

"It should be here again in about seven weeks, but I need to look at the papers that were on my boat."

Sanchez sent a man to get any papers that were in the evidence box for this case. The man returned a few minutes later with a briefcase and handed it to Sanchez. "There you are, see what you have there," Sanchez said as he handed over the papers from the case.

After looking at a paper the boat owner said, "That's it, it's in code but it tells me that the next time it should be back is fifty-three days time. I should say there have been two occasions when it has been late. The shipping list will give the date."

"Right, we shall have to put you back in custody until we decide what we do next." Sanchez sent two of his men to accompany the boat owner back to Belgium for the time being; he might be useful again later.

After talking together Taylor, Rebecca and Sanchez decided that this was a job for EU Foreign Office. All details were sent to the Paris HQ for their onward transmission to the EU. As a belt and braces approach Sanchez also decided to emulate the Sea Princess occasion where they met the boat with a team of people. He was concerned whether the Mexican Government would manage to prevent the drugs being put on board. There was plenty of time to arrange any reception of the ship by the EUDforce.

Sanchez allowed himself time to reflect upon the progress as a whole. He knew that a massive hole had been made in the general illegal drugs business. There were so many dealers and suppliers caught that an old prison in Yorkshire had to be refurbished to accommodate some of them. The existing prisons took a lot of them but were pushed to take them all.

The intelligence team in cooperation with Scotland Yard had made it possible to retrieve tons of drugs. The EU Foreign Office now had a ship from Mexico, another from Pakistan and details of the heroin estate in Afghanistan.

Sanchez realised that there were no other items under his direct control that would give the result he wanted: access to the drug barons. He realised however, he was causing huge aggravation for these people and they were losing millions of dollars.

Thoughts of Rebecca washed over his mind; they both had been so busy that a repeat of their dinner and walk had not been possible. Sanchez decided that time had to be made for another meeting with Rebecca and talked to her immediately.

"Rebecca, let's go out to dinner again tonight, can you make it?"

"Yes Pedro of course. What time?"

"Say seven-thirty outside your hotel, is that ok?"

"That's ok Pedro," she answered.

The official car that Sanchez rarely used pulled up at Rebecca's hotel promptly at seven thirty with Sanchez already in it. He got out and escorted Rebecca into the car.

"Where to Sir?" asked the driver.

"That restaurant where you took me for the meeting with the Minister, do you remember?"

"Oh yes Sir, I remember."

The car sped off and Rebecca and Sanchez settled down in the back seat for the thirty-minute drive to the restaurant. Sanchez chose this place because he had liked very much the food and the service; the décor was modern without being garish. There was also a small dance floor and he wanted to have Rebecca in his arms again. It was a really pleasant place with soft music in the background and dance music at intervals.

They enjoyed an excellent dinner with wine and danced a while. When they were ready to go Sanchez asked the driver to take them down to the river so they could walk back together to the hotel. Sanchez was surprised and delighted when Rebecca, after cuddling close as they walked for a while, looked up and said quietly," Pedro lets go back to my hotel room." They were situated in separate hotels until permanent accommodation could be arranged for all the various staff.

They arrived in Rebecca's room and Pedro kissed her passionately. They raced to get their clothes off and soon were on the bed. They kissed with continuing passion and soon Pedro's manhood found the softness between her thighs. They worked together until an explosion of satisfaction enveloped them both. Finally they separated and lay breathless.

Sanchez rolled over to face Rebecca and said simply," Will you marry me?"

Rebecca looked at him and said," Yes, on one condition."

"Name it," replied Sanchez.

"I do not want to leave the police service, have you any difficulty with that?"

He replied immediately, "No, of course not, you're too good to leave anyway!" Rebecca laughed and cuddled in closer to Sanchez. They slept together that night and in the morning discussed marriage plans.

"Do you think we can still work together once we are married or will there be any problem," asked Rebecca.

"I am sure my boss will not allow any problems to upset things. I am not worried about it," answered Sanchez.

Their experience this night encouraged them to have many such nights and it became obvious to many of the staff that a romance was happening in their midst.

15

Talbot had passed all the information about the 'Eastern Gem' from Pakistan and the 'Rainbow' from Mexico to the EU Foreign Office. He also gave them a copy of the letter from Mohammed about the heroin estate in Afghanistan.

The fact that there was now a single voice from the EU did not make it any easier in cases like this. There was no corresponding EU Embassy in each country, so one of the existing Ambassadors from a designated country within the EU acted for the EU. Talbot thought it was a messy arrangement but he had no say in the matter; he did however mention it to the Chairman of the EU Committee to whom he reported. He did not obtain a useful answer although he suspected that the Chairman also did not think much of the arrangement.

In Mexico, the designated Embassy was the German one so all the information about the ship and drugs finished up in their hands. The German Ambassador read the report carefully; he did not want to appear to tell the Mexicans how to run their security and drug busting arrangements. He did think they ought to be pleased to find out more about what was going on in their own country. He knew the Minister for internal affairs reasonably well but he thought the Mexicans were a bit excitable.

Being a very cautious individual he decided to talk round this particular problem until the right moment arrived to mention it. He rang the Minister and said he would like to have a chat as they had not talked for some time. The Minister received the request with pleasure and agreed a date.

On the agreed day, the Ambassador called for his car and driver to take him to the Minister. He was ushered into the Minister's office and greeted warmly. "Good morning Wolfgang, it is good to see you again. I hope you are well, do sit down please."

"Thank you Felipe, yes I am very well, how are the children, is it three or four?"

"Oh they are fine and its four now," replied the Minister.

"My word, how time flies. Your eldest must be thirteen."

"I agree Wolfgang, it only seems yesterday since the youngest was born and she is now three, and yes the boy is thirteen. Anyway how is your wife, she was not very well the last time we met?" asked the Minister.

"Yes she was unwell for a time but she is quite ok now thank you Felipe."

The Minister asked, "Will you take coffee Wolfgang?"

"Thank you, that would be very welcome," the Ambassador replied.

The Minister rang for coffee and a tray was brought in with coffee and biscuits. They continued small talk over the refreshments for a time then the Ambassador asked about the illegal drugs trade. "Are you having much trouble with this?"

"Oh still all the usual, we stop one lot and another appears. How is the new EUDforce doing? Has it brought any success so far?"

"Yes," replied the Ambassador, "We started in the UK and we have caught a lot of people and recovered great quantities of drugs. I think it is going very well."

"That is good," said the Minister, "are there any drugs identified as from Mexico?"

The Ambassador thought to himself, you know very well that many drugs come out of your country. However, he felt this was the opportunity for him to mention the 'Rainbow'. He delicately suggested that there was suspicion about drugs on a ship or two from Mexico.

The Minister seemed interested and asked, "Any particular ship, Wolfgang?"

The Ambassador appeared to think for a moment, "Yes, I think it was called the 'Rainbow' or a name like it."

"Perhaps you can give me more details, Wolfgang. We should look into this."

"All we know is that it plies regularly between here and the UK."

"Well I can find out when it sails and arrange for a search," said the Minister.

"That would be excellent Felipe. I hope you have some success." The Ambassador then added, "I wonder whether you might be able to find the source of the drugs from this search but I'm not sure how difficult that would be."

The Minister made no immediate reply, as he was busy telephoning one of his people to look into the matter. He then spoke again after his phone call. "I will let you know what happens Wolfgang, but I expect it will take a little time."

"Of course," replied the Ambassador.

After a few more pleasantries the Ambassador took his leave and went back to his Embassy. He duly reported to the EU Foreign Office and said he believed something would be done. He also promised to update them when he had news that was more definite.

In Pakistan, the French Ambassador was the representative for the EU and he read the information about the 'Eastern Gem'. He also studied a copy of the letter from Mohammed and the details of the place to which Omar flew the heroin and met the mule trains. He thought the meeting he must have with the Foreign Minister might be a tricky one. He knew the Pakistan government was very touchy about any implication that they had missed something within their control of illegal drugs or security. It was obvious that they had huge problems because of natural disasters.

In the North, there were still large numbers of people without homes due to earthquakes and floods. This took up a considerable amount of government time and many countries were involved in helping them.

It was a week earlier that the French Ambassador had a meeting with his opposite number, the Foreign Minister. After the initial conversation, the Ambassador asked whether his country could offer any more help. The Minister replied, "No thank you, we now have vast stocks of food, medical supplies etc. but the problem is still the distribution. We appreciate the help you are already giving with your helicopters."

The Ambassador nodded as the Minister added, "The area is vast as you know, and I am afraid it will take time."

The Ambassador nodded again and said, "I understand. We are all extremely sorry for the people involved and you know that we have supplied nearly all our helicopters."

"My dear friend, I assure you that we are very conscious of your tremendous help, but there is nothing else you can do."

The Ambassador thought for a moment, he would have to broach the drugs subject now, offend or please. "There is one thing Minister I meant to say, about our work in the UK with our new EUDforce. We have information that may be useful to you although I quite understand that you have many other priorities." The Minister was interested and listened carefully as the Ambassador told him about the 'Eastern Gem' and the details of Mohammed's letter.

After the Minister had read the letter himself, he remarked, "What a thorough explanation from the writer, who is he?"

"Apparently he was a foreman on the estate," replied the Ambassador.

The Minister looked thoughtful for some time before he resumed the conversation, "As you will know we have to juggle with many problems at the same time but I am sure we should look into this. Thank you for the information."

The Minister looked again at the copy of the letter from Mohammed and remarked, "He has certainly made a good job of detailing the estate and the place where the heroin is transferred. Leave it with me."

The Ambassador left after a few minutes and, when back in his Embassy, reported to the EU.

In Afghanistan the British Ambassador was on a similar mission dealing with the letter from Mohammed.

He thought that for an obviously uneducated man Mohammed had made a good job of describing the heroin estate. He thought it would be a good idea to have this man brought over to the UK sometime. He deserved recognition for the detailed way the letter had been produced.

Now he had to persuade the Afghanistan government to do something about it all. He made an appointment to see the Minister of the Interior and, a few days later, was welcomed into his office. The Minister was younger than the Ambassador was and the welcome was warm.

After conversing a little, the Minister asked, "Now Sir Hugh, I believe you have a particular subject you wish to discuss with me."

"Yes, I have information about a heroin estate that may interest you. It is clearly identified in this letter" He handed the Minister a copy of the letter that Mohammed had sent and said, "We would, of course, like to close it but that would be up to you to decide. You will also see there is information in the letter about the heroin route to and out of Pakistan."

The Minister looked at the Ambassador and said, "I suspect we shall find a can of worms here, this place must have been protected; there is still corruption to weed out. The Ambassador stayed silent, it was not his place to agree about any corruption. The Minister added, "Leave the matter with me; I'll contact you as soon as I can figure out what is going on. I'm sure you understand that with this new government there are many things to be sorted out."

The Ambassador smiled and nodded, he did not want to say too much. He left and a report was sent to the EU Foreign Office via the safe messaging service which was automatically encrypted. He told them that he had made contact and as soon as more news evolved, he would be in touch again.

It was a week later that the Minister rang him. "If you would like to join me for tea I will tell you about the letter and the estate."

Sir Hugh Penfold, the British Ambassador, agreed to go and was soon seated in the Minister's office enjoying a cup of tea. He also was anxious to know about the estate. The Minister said, "It pains me to say this but I have unearthed a veritable web of corruption around this estate. I have now put into action a cleansing of the people involved and I am ashamed to say there are many." The Ambassador kept silent as he suspected there was more to come.

The Minister continued, "I hope that within a few more days my initial work will be complete and a new set of police installed. I have also learned that the original owner an Omar Rahim has died and that his nephew now runs the estate. I think he will soon have an unpleasant surprise."

The Ambassador thanked the Minister for the information, returned to his Embassy and reported his news.

Three days later the Ambassador received a brief message from the Minister. "We are all set for a raid the day after tomorrow. I will tell you about it when we have finished." The Minister could not tell the Ambassador all that he had found out in looking at the police and others who had protected the heroin estate for so long.

The Ambassador was pleased to hear this latest news; he knew that the EUDforce would be very satisfied if this estate could be closed down. Another report went to the EU. He admired the work that the EUDforce was doing and had met Talbot in England.

The Afghan Minister of the Interior had a battle royal with the various people around the protection of the heroin estate. The army was called in, to clear out some of the higher ranks of the police. He would have been ashamed to give all the details to the Ambassador. Now all was ready for the final push to eliminate another evil.

As usual things did not turn out quite as expected; success was mixed with failure.

16

Hamid and Ahmed were having breakfast on the large terrace surrounding the mansion. There was not much to do today as Hamid was up to date with all his heroin production and Ahmed's accounts were always in good order, so they relaxed and chatted about everything in general. They also reminisced about Omar. Under Hamid's rule, there had been dramatic changes in the estate.

Neat log cabins, with proper bedrooms and separate living rooms had replaced the workers terrible accommodation. Compared with those paid previously, wages had increased substantially. There was no more cruelty and the guards were under strict instructions that any workers who attempted to run away must be brought to Hamid unharmed. He would then find out the problem and try to resolve it.

The same thing applied to casual intruders; the old days of shoot first were over. Strangely enough, the guards were given no instructions about what they should do if attacked. Omar had always guarded the estate, not relying only on the guards, but by bribing the police and others. The chance of an attack on the estate must always have existed, if one of their corrupt protectors reneged on agreements: this seemed an important omission even though it is doubtful whether such knowledge would help. Hamid was liked by his employees and there was little trouble. The betterment of their lives led to vastly increased production so Hamid was pleased with the result.

This day of relaxation was fine, not a cloud in the sky, hot and with little breeze; the two men drank their coffee and thought that life was good. The atmosphere was quiet and occasional sounds of work in the valley could be heard. Hamid leaned back in his comfortable wicker chair and marvelled at the turn of events and the disparity between this life and his old one. His main disappointment was that he had been unable to persuade his wife to join him. She had entreated him on several occasions to come home but Hamid did not want to leave, especially now that the estate belonged to him.

While he mused, half asleep, he thought he could hear a series of short sharp cracking sounds and wondered what it could be. He turned to Ahmed and asked, "Did you hear that Ahmed?"

There was a short interval while Ahmed listened. "I heard something different from the usual sounds in the valley Hamid but I don't know what it is." They listened again and this time Ahmed said, "I believe those are shots, what can be happening?" He hurriedly got his field glasses and scanned the valley and the fields outside of the mansion grounds. Ahmed was usually a very placid individual but what he saw drove him to instant action. He spoke sharply, "Go into your study now and please don't argue. I will follow you very shortly: there is great danger"

Hamid trusted Ahmed implicitly and immediately obeyed him. As he moved into the study there were sounds of bullets hitting the outside of the building and Hamid realised that Ahmed had probably saved his life.

Ahmed rushed into his office and picked up a briefcase, which held their identity papers and other important documents together with a large quantity of Afghanis. The documents also included details of the savings accounts, chequebooks and other personal papers. Omar had always insisted that they should be ready for immediate flight as he suspected that one day his protection process would fail through one reason or another. Ahmed had continues the practice and its use was now called into action. In such an emergency, there was no time to waste. Ahmed nearly bumped into Hamid as he rushed back into the study. "Come Hamid, help me with this bookcase. I will explain later."

They both pulled hard on one of the bookcases and it moved around to reveal a heavy wooden door. Ahmed pulled a bunch of keys from the briefcase and chose a key with a red marker on it. He opened the door and once they were through Ahmed and Hamid rolled the bookcase back into position, relocked the door and led the way down some stairs and through a passage. After about ten metres they came to another door, this time made of heavy steel. Ahmed unlocked it with a key from the bunch and they slipped through. They relocked it and moved on.

The steel door was the entrance to a series of shallow caves, which went on for a distance of probably fifty metres. They had to walk doubled up through these caves and then came to a small room-like cave, the exit of which was another closed steel door. Again, Ahmed found a key from the briefcase and this time the door revealed a narrow exit to the outside.

They exited very warily as they were not too far from the mansion, but they were in a narrow defile where they were hidden from view. They travelled on for some thousand metres and emerged well away from sight of their previous home.

They rested here for a few minutes and Ahmed told Hamid what he had seen and why they had fled.

"What I saw Hamid, were more than thirty police and also some army units. I am afraid that our life on the estate is finished and we are free only due to the foresight of your uncle. He told me that when he was younger he had found the cave complex and decided to prepare an escape route in case the police changed their minds about the elaborate protection he paid for. I have not been down there before but I did not forget the description he gave me." Ahmed continued after a pause, as he had not quite recovered from his exertions, "Now we must get away as far as possible and try to get some transport." They then set off for the nearest village, some five kilometres away.

At the estate, the police soon overcame the limited resistance of the guards who were handcuffed and taken away. The workers in the valley were rounded up and a decision on what to do with them was to be taken later. When the police learned of the prison like life that the workers experienced they were not so intent on punishing them; it was the owners they were after. In the meantime, the workers were taken to the police headquarters and put into a large, safe room.

The police soon arrived at the house but found no one there. The policeman in charge ordered his men to go through the place in detail. It took two days to search the mansion and outbuildings properly and found nothing of any importance that gave more clues about the inhabitants.

It was by chance that an observant policeman saw a discrepancy in the line up of the bookcases. One stood a little proud of the others. With the help of a colleague, the officer finally found the secret of the door behind the bookcase.

The wooden door was soon broken through and then they found the steel door down the passage. This was a different proposition to the wooden one and it took five hours of hard work to break it down. Two police went in to the cave complex but found nothing. After consultations the police were not even sure whether the escape route had been used or not as there was no clear evidence, merely the fact that it existed. The police were not aware that Omar had died as this bit of information was omitted from their brief; they did not know that his nephew was running the estate.

When they decided to search the nearby towns it was therefore Omar they were looking for, not Hamid, and they knew nothing of Ahmed.

Hamid managed to persuade a farmer, after a few Afghanis had changed hands, to give them a lift into a small town. They thanked the farmer and looked around for somewhere to purchase a vehicle. After a questioning many inhabitants they were told of a garage-like place where they might get a car or old van. They finally bought a very old car and some petrol and made their way to Meyhabul where Hamid's wife still lived.

They wondered whether the petrol would be enough, as they could not buy many litres and on their journey they were on tenterhooks as to whether the petrol would last; if not it would be a long walk and Ahmed was not really fit for much exercise. It was late afternoon when Hamid knocked gently at the door of his old home.

The door soon opened and his wife appeared. She was shocked to see Hamid and gasped in amazement. "What are you doing here; I thought you were at your Uncle's place?"

"It's a long story," Hamid said as he kissed his wife and hugged her for a long time. He promised, "I'll tell you all about it in due course." His wife said,

"I expect you are hungry, you look tired as well."

Hamid agreed, adding, "Let me introduce my friend Ahmed, he was the estate manager." After Hamid's wife acknowledged Ahmed, the two men sat down while she prepared a meal.

The two men ate quickly as they were very hungry and afterwards, while they enjoyed a cup of tea and some plain biscuits Hamid told his story. His wife sat open-mouthed as the story progressed. "So there you are, that is it. That is why we are here."

"Will the police be looking for you?" his wife asked.

"No I don't think there is any chance of that," said Ahmed, "In any case I suspect they may be looking for the uncle not Hamid and they do not know much about me.

Hamid's wife was not poor because Hamid had sent her money on a regular basis. Now, Hamid thought, they could start afresh; perhaps buy one of those big houses near the Mayor.

Back on the heroin estate, the search of Omar's, then Hamid's mansion was completed and the police moved in to the shallow valley again to search for any more evidence. They destroyed the growing poppy crops and set fire to the log cabins. The aeroplane was flown out to a police airfield probably to be sold after being treated as evidence. They did not destroy the mansion but there was some looting of furniture and effects, shared out, no doubt, among the higher ranks of the police. Corruption takes a long time to disappear completely.

The horses found their way to the quite luxurious home of the Chief of Police. They had no idea where Hamid was, all they found were a few servants who had no idea where their master had gone. None of them told the police of the change of ownership.

The police tried to find out where any money was hidden or banked but to no avail. The case was closed and the mansion gradually fell in to disrepair.

A month had passed since Hamid returned to Meyhabul. He spoke to Ahmed about the possibility of moving to a better house. "What do you think Ahmed?"

"It's up to you Hamid, perhaps you would rather get a house for the two of you, I can soon find a house somewhere."

Hamid was quite indignant, "After what we have been through together I would not think of you getting another place. We would like you to live with us."

Ahmed was touched by Hamid's statement and tears appeared in his eyes. Hamid saw the tears and gave Ahmed a big hug. He said, "We will start looking tomorrow." He then thought for a moment and said, "But how do we pay for it, we may not have enough Afghanis to buy a house and live properly at the same time."

Ahmed said, "I had contacts before who would arrange to change cheques when I wanted Afghanis but of course they are not available anymore."

Hamid said, "I wonder if the moneylender could help us, he must be quite a big man in the money business." Hamid went to see the moneylender who welcomed him warmly. They had a long talk and Hamid told him what had happened.

"I think you have been very lucky Hamid, I hope you will settle down now and enjoy life."

Hamid assured him that was his intention and brought up the subject of the difficulty of the Afghanis. He said that he had plenty of money in the bank but could not get at it in the form of Afghan currency. The estate had always plenty of Afghanis as well as the dollars in the Western bank but the estate was no more. The moneylender replied that this was not a problem; he could change any cheque for them. Hamid wondered how he could do this; he obviously had plenty of contacts somewhere.   Hamid went back and told Ahmed the good news. After looking around, they settled on a spacious house not far from the moneylender. Hamid of course went to see his old boss on a regular basis. The stammering Hamid who had first approached the moneylender was now a confident man and the moneylender saw a great change in him.

One day Hamid thought how his uncle had felt about family when he was unwell. As Hamid had only one relative left, his cousin Abdullah, he decided to write to him and if convenient to visit him. He did not know how to address the letter but he would do the same as Omar had done and write to the Mayor of Ghazi rat. He sent a simple message asking Abdullah whether he could come and visit for say two weeks.

The Mayor of Ghazi rat, when he received the letter wondered how he would get it to Abdullah. He had never visited the village and it seemed to be difficult to find. He would have to wait until Abdullah or one of his men came into Ghazi rat. He knew that the villager would go to the main store so he left a note for someone to contact him.

Hamid had no idea that once again he had set in train a series of events that might not be good for him.

17

Abdullah and his Second in Command of the village in the hills had opened the village storage room built into the rock.

It held all their stocks of staple food, which Abdullah shared out each week. The village existed as a sort of commune where they shared all this food; many other items in the village were common property. The elders of the village had decided this way of life many years ago and it still worked. It would not be correct to say that all the villagers approved but they would probably find it difficult to live outside the village. None had any particular skills. Their only skill lay in planting poppies and extracting opium from the seedpods.

In the storage room, which was built into the side of a hill, was a very thick wooden safe; the two men had come to check the contents. After opening the safe, they counted the number of Afghanis, saved to purchase food and other essentials.

What they found would have to last until the opium from the next poppy crop. They carefully counted the money and then Abdullah equally carefully divided the stack into a number of piles; each pile was enough to provide a reasonable life for all, for a week. He then counted the piles and shook his head. "There are more weeks than piles of Afghanis," he said to his companion.

"What shall we do," asked his second in command.

"The piles have to be made smaller or we have to get some more Afghanis, and I cannot see how we can do that," replied Abdullah. His assistant sat down with his head in his hands and Abdullah sat by his side.

"Is this all due to the price drop Abdullah?"

"Well, I did get a little more as you know, but obviously not enough," replied Abdullah.

Both men saw an impossible situation and sat thinking about it. They had been cogitating for several minutes when there was a tentative voice from outside.

"Abdullah, can I talk to you?"

Abdullah did not like interruptions while he was checking the contents of the store and it was unusual for this to occur. However, on this occasion he answered, "Yes, what do you want?"

"I am sorry to disturb you but you may want to know that the men are back from Ghazi rat and there is a letter for you."

"All right, I will come out in a moment or so."

He turned to his companion, "Let us lock up and see what this is all about, we can come back later." He also thought, who on earth would write to me? With that thought, Abdullah put the money in the safe, locked the safe door and then went outside and locked the store.

He was among a handful of men in the village who could read and write. His second in command together with four other men and one woman were able to do so. Abdullah greeted the men who had returned from getting supplies, asked them if they had experienced any problems, and accepted the letter. He took it to his home and read it carefully. While he could read quite adequately, he was slow in doing so.

The letter interested him greatly; his cousin Hamid, wanted to come and see him. He wondered why now, after all these years but thought, still it would be nice. As far as he knew Hamid was the only relative he had. He wrote the next day saying that he would like to see Hamid and for Hamid to let him know when he could come. After writing, he had to wait until he could get the letter to Ghazi rat.

It was another ten days before one of his men went to Ghazi rat for a few supplies that were omitted on the last visit.

Correspondence was in any case a long job as the post was slow and not very efficient. He knew he would have to meet him, either through the hills route or the valley path.

Weeks passed and his men brought him another letter. This time Hamid told him that he would reach Ghazi rat on a certain date. The date was only four days from the date that Abdullah received the letter. He decided to use the hills route and arranged to take one of the experienced men with him. He did not want to make a slip like he did before when he was notified that he had been trailed.

The next morning the two men set off for the town and took their time, as they did not need to get there until the date as given in the letter. They were careful as they approached the town, as they did not want to meet anybody from the authorities. They arrived safely, two days after they had left home and their arrival was quite uneventful. There was a very cheap lodging house where they could stay for the night.

After finding the house, a meal was very welcome. An hour after eating they decided to retire for the night. Abdullah was quietly excited at the prospect of seeing his cousin.

Hamid and Ahmed arrived by bus, after a dirty and uncomfortable journey taking three hours. They looked around at the so-called bus station but there was no sign of Abdullah. They walked around to relieve the stiffness in their muscles from the journey. A few minutes later Hamid saw two men walking quickly towards him. He thought he recognized Abdullah but was not sure until the men came closer. He saw a middle-aged man who he was now quite sure was Abdullah even after the years apart.

Hamid was the first to speak, "Abdullah?"

Abdullah replied, "Yes, I am Abdullah, how are you, Cousin?"

As they shook hands warmly and gave each other a hug, Hamid answered, "I am very well; you look good, are you ok?"

Abdullah said, "I am fine thanks."

His cousin introduced Ahmed. "I want you to meet my very good friend, Ahmed, we have worked together for some time." Abdullah acknowledged Ahmed and they shook hands.

Abdullah suggested that Hamid and Ahmed might like a meal before they set off for the village. The two visitors agreed and said they were both hungry. Abdullah knew that the general store where he sold his opium would provide a meal and led them to the place. By noon they were on their way; Abdullah had filled up water bottles and bought some food for the journey.

He explained to Hamid that the journey was long and the going rough so it was wise to go slowly. There was a little trouble as they progressed; Ahmed developed blisters on his feet, which required attention. Neither Hamid nor Ahmed had shoes that were really fit for such a journey. They reached the village the next day having had a sleep on the way and the villagers were quite excited to see strangers; this was a rare event.

Hamid and Ahmed were introduced to everyone and it was decided to hold a dinner that night to celebrate the arrival. Abdullah was slightly concerned at the usage of resources but then thought there was little he could do so he might as well enjoy the celebration.

Abdullah and Hamid spent a long time conversing about their childhood, and how their lives had developed afterwards. Ahmed spent time with the second in command of the village and soon learned that the money situation was tight due to the opium price not being strong enough. Ahmed thought he would have a word with Hamid about it: he was sure they could help.

The celebration was a great success and Hamid and Ahmed went to bed that night having thoroughly enjoyed themselves. It was the next day when Ahmed told Hamid of his conversation and learning of the shortage of money.

Hamid said, "These are proud people; we must be careful how we do it."

"I understand Hamid, I think I will leave it to you to talk to Abdullah."

It was later that day that Hamid felt he should talk to Abdullah. He started by talking about his experiences with heroin prices and their variations. Abdullah spoke about how the low price of the opium was making life difficult for the village. He understood that many people had to make money in the movement of the opium to its final destination but thought his share was too small.

"I know that you are a proud man, my cousin, but I have a suggestion that may help all of you." Abdullah was interested in what Hamid had to say and nodded his head for Hamid to continue. "What I thought was this; I will lend you some money." Abdullah started to object but Hamid said, "You have not heard it all yet."

Abdullah apologised and Hamid continued, "I will lend you some money to tide you over until you have opium to sell again. I will then ensure that the opium price is much better than you have been getting: you will then be able to pay me back. Also I shall not be in any hurry so there will be no strain on you"

Abdullah sat and thought for some time and said, "How can you afford to buy at a better price?"

"You must leave that to me Abdullah, don't forget I have been in this business and know my way around the market."

Abdullah thought again then said, "I do not like to borrow but I can see it may be the only way especially if the opium price can be improved."

"Is that agreed then?" asked Hamid.

"Yes I agree, and it is most kind of you to do this."

"No it is not kind, what is family for?" said Hamid. He continued, "Right then, how much do you need?"

"I will talk with my second in command and let you know tomorrow and thank you again."

Hamid put his arm round Abdullah's shoulder and said again, "I said before, what is family for, if we cannot help one another the world has gone crazy."

Abdullah smiled and walked away.

Hamid had been thinking about the loan and what he intended to do was simple. He would make an arrangement so that Abdullah could still take the opium to Ghazi rat and sell it to the 'business' and he simply paid any difference to make up a good price. He knew Abdullah would be able to save money out of the difference. In the end it would only cost Hamid the difference money. He could easily do this for several years and then who knows what could happen?

Hamid was correct in thinking that no one could tell what fate had in store for the village and indeed for himself.

In Ghazi rat the policeman who had looked at the village several weeks ago learned that he soon would be able to use the helicopter again.

He had this niggling thought from his previous flight that he had seen a rock move. He had not told anyone in case he was ridiculed, but he just had this feeling. Next time he would ask the pilot to go lower or try to land somewhere. Fate might have a surprise for him as well: it might not be pleasant.

18

Sanchez and Rebecca were married at a registry office in London and forty-one guests plus two children attended. The wedding and reception were simple; unfortunately neither had any family who could attend. Sanchez had his best man and three other friends from Spain.

Seven friends of Rebecca came and she had two little bridesmaids. In addition there were twenty-eight people from the EUDforce including Maurice Talbot. The Commissioner from Scotland Yard and his wife also attended.

Rebecca was dressed in white in a very fashionable outfit that Sanchez thought was highly suited to her exquisite figure. His rank was equivalent to a Commander in the UK and he wore his police dress-uniform from Spain.

They undoubtedly looked a very fine couple and the speeches reflected the fact. The Commissioner spoke warmly about Sanchez and congratulated them both saying what a handsome couple they made, "Ideally suited to one another," he exclaimed.

The reception was at the hotel where Rebecca was staying and was enjoyed by all; even the Commissioner was tempted to have a dance with the bride. It was the first dance he had tried for years and he managed it without treading on the bride's toes, at least that is what she said. The reception was in the afternoon and afterwards, in the evening, there was a disco, which was attended by more of their friends and EUDforce people.

Sanchez and Rebecca slipped away while the evening enjoyment was still going on and caught the Euro Express to Paris. They stayed there for the night and then hired a car to take them to their final destination in Saumur on the river Loire. The honeymoon was a brief one, eight days in all, in a comfortable hotel right by the river.

As Rebecca was fond of horses they attended the training establishment in Saumur where the finest horse riders in France came to perfect their riding skills. They were fortunate in that they arrived at the same time as an exhibition of riding was being shown to some foreign dignitaries. Rebecca wandered about the place looking at the many horses in their stalls, each with details of birth, age etc.

Sanchez was particularly interested in the period in history from Franco's regime through to the Second World War. It was a good opportunity for him to go to the tank museum in Saumur, where there were examples of World War Two tanks, including Russian and German types. There was one example where a tank had a large shell buried in its side. It would not have been a 'French' trip without having a wander round some wineries and of course sampling the wine.

The time seemed to fly and so it was soon necessary to return to London and start work again.

Talbot had returned to France until Sanchez came back and then flew to the UK for a meeting with him. They wanted to examine the total progress to date and learn any lessons for the future. It was a long session looking at all the results to date. The administrator, who had been with Sanchez from the start, compiled these for them. The Commissioner had recommended him when Sanchez first arrived in the UK. He had proved to be invaluable and Sanchez realised he could not have progressed so well without him.

In the UK, there had been significant advances; hundreds of various levels of suppliers were in jail and a few had new identities – allocated because of the outstanding amount and usefulness of their information. The amount of drugs captured and destroyed was an all-time record and the amount on the streets was definitely diminishing as big suppliers could not sell: the drugs were being seized before they could be distributed. Drug prices were sky-high due to the shortage.

The rehabilitation teams that had been working all the time Sanchez had been in the UK reported good progress but there was a long way to go. It took a long time to get people off the habit.

The intelligence team together with the Yard team had done very good work leading to dozens of referrals to the EU Foreign Office for action in illegal drug producing countries. Sanchez was seeing, as a backdrop to all that, an improvement in cooperation between the UK and foreign police forces.

It had always existed of course but with three factors now increasing the efficiency. First, there was what the UK was doing, secondly the efforts of central headquarters in Paris and thirdly the pressure put on other countries by the EU Foreign Office.

Although Talbot had disliked having no corresponding Ambassador in the various countries the system seemed to work well enough. Sanchez and Talbot agreed that all this was very successful and in the case of the UK, they had adhered to the EU directive. However, they agreed that good as all these results appeared to be, breaking the main suppliers on their home ground was difficult. If these suppliers had no customers then this was a success.

They expected that, as they went through the other EU countries, more information would be forthcoming and more main suppliers put out of business. Talbot said it was known already that more drugs were now being diverted from the UK to the USA. He had also heard that the USA was interested in the European experience, although they might find it difficult to start a similar scheme.

Talbot asked Sanchez, "Do you think you should now move on to another country Pedro?"

Sanchez thought for a moment then said, "I certainly think the time is approaching for me to leave the UK end of the business to Roger Taylor who is doing a good job as the head here." Sanchez continued, "From the experience here I am not sure that I made a great deal of difference in choosing the people."

Talbot looked surprised and said, "What do you mean?"

"I think what we are doing is wrong, in the sense that it is too slow. We cannot do this country by country as the EU committee suggested. We have to get each country to pick the men and women they think can do the job. After being brought over here for a rapid period of experience, they could be sent back to get on with it. If time permits, they could also go on the course in France. I can then coordinate the heads of each country as your second in command; furthermore I can look, over time, at the efficacy of the individual staff."

This statement by Sanchez made a lot of sense thought Talbot. He also had been concerned at the slowness of the overall method but not at Sanchez's effort in the UK. He would have to explain this to the Committee, as they had seemed set on this country-by-country approach.

Talbot managed to speak to the committee chairman, a week after his conversation with Sanchez. He sensed opposition immediately and suspected that he was the one who had dreamt up the serial approach. "I would suggest Sir that in this way we will be able to combine a more speedy approach to eventually covering Europe and that Sanchez will still be able to select and reselect all the staff."

The last bit of his statement sounded all right to Talbot although he was not sure how the chairman would view it.

The chairman thought about the suggestion for a full minute then said, "Are you sure that Sanchez can do this?"

"Oh yes Sir, he can do a better job if we adopt this approach; he can coordinate the activities in each country while they are progressing the work."

"I see," replied the chairman. "Well, if you are confident we will do it."

Talbot spoke to Sanchez immediately on the video link, "Pedro, the chairman has bought your suggestion, you can get cracking now."

Sanchez was obviously pleased, "OK Maurice that is great news, as you say, I can indeed get cracking and you can be sure I will."

Talbot said, "Glad to hear it my boy, now there is another matter which has come down from the Committee. It concerns the widening of the job specification, firstly of course in the UK. It is to include the selling of illegal drugs on the internet. As you know, there are all sorts of chemical concoctions available. There is a lot of work going on already in this field; you will help if the opportunity arises for using your particular way of doing things." Talbot continued, "In addition, the question of UK made artificial illegal drugs should also be included immediately."

Talbot then mentioned the man, Mohammed who had given such valuable information to the EUDforce.

"The subject of bringing Mohammed to the UK was raised by the chairman. I said that we both thought it was a great idea and he will put the matter up to the EU committee."

A week later Talbot spoke to Sanchez again and told him Mohammed would be brought to the UK and rewarded for his efforts. Mohammed would then realise how he had changed events in Afghanistan and Pakistan.

Sanchez asked Roger Taylor to meet him and told him of the extra work that Talbot had mentioned. He explained that the first job was to evolve a plan to see what the existing staff could do and whether extra resources would be required. He also said that cooperation with other countries would be necessary and that the Paris HQ could be very much involved due to its large computer and administrative facilities. Taylor went away suitably impressed with the very large task that was in front of him. Ostensibly, the problem applied to the UK but Taylor knew that Sanchez was right; they would need enormous co-ordinated efforts from Paris.

He sat down with senior colleagues to try to put into context the requirements of the job. Undoubtedly, the internet was going to be a problem; there was no way that one country could solve the problem, it would be worldwide. After a long meeting, Taylor evolved a plan of sorts; he was not wholly satisfied but it was a start.

Without doubt, more resources were needed, especially to combat the internet trade; it seemed an almost impossible problem.

19

In Ghazi rat the opportunity came at last for the police inspector to revisit Abdullah's village by helicopter. He had waited a long time since feeling there was something wrong about his last visit. The helicopter pilot however was not too happy about this next mission. He had been asked to take the same policeman over the hill village, as he had before. In itself, this was not a problem but since learning that he could have the helicopter again, the man seemed obsessed. He was sure he had seen a rock move and was now telling all his colleagues about it; previously he had kept quiet.

His colleagues were laughing at him behind his back and kidding the pilot that he was going to have a hard time. This did not improve the pilot's feelings about the problems he might have; he certainly did not want to lose his life for a look at a village. What was worse from the pilot's point of view was the policeman's stated intention of getting as near to the ground as possible; the pilot thought he had done this already.   The policeman spoke to the pilot with a passion that was not normal, all about this rock that moved and how he was sure they would see it this time. On the previous trip, they had been close to the ground and the pilot was not keen on going any nearer. There was no place to land easily unless he tried for the large field and he was not too keen on that. He could not tell what the contour of the ground was like and he had no wish to tip the machine over. There was little doubt that the pilot was a worried man.

The time arrived for them to set off for the village and when the villagers heard the sound, some distance away, they adopted the same procedure as before; the single toned horn was blown and the whole village closed down and appeared empty.

Abdullah, his second in command and Hamid were in the opium shed and the raffia shutters were pulled down very quickly, after hearing the horn. The village looked dead, as it was supposed to look.

As the helicopter drew nearer the policeman grew excited; he craned his head out of the small window in the machine and looked intently at the ground. They first did a circuit round the field; the huts and the whole village looked empty and the pilot said, "I can't see any sign of life sir, It must be empty."

"There is something there, I am sure," commented the policeman, "go round again and get lower."

The pilot flew round again just a little lower than before and certainly as low as he thought it safe to be. The pilot was getting extremely concerned at the voice of the policeman; it was hysterical now, and he was trying to get hold of the controls. "All right sir, let go, I'll try and get lower."

They flew round again even lower than before with the policeman nearly out of the window in his anxiety to look at the village. He withdrew from the window and screamed at the pilot, "There is movement I am certain, go lower," He again tried to grab the controls while shouting at the pilot. The pilot was now fighting to keep the helicopter steady as they continued to struggle.

The pilot shouted, "Let go, let go you fool," He desperately tried to keep the helicopter flying safely. The two men continued to struggle with the controls as the helicopter moved in an unnatural and jerky manner. Now the pilot was punching the policeman, trying to regain some control. He could see it was nearly too late and shouted again for the policeman to let him fly the machine without interference. The policeman took no notice and screamed hysterically,

"I want to look."

By now the helicopter was rocking uncontrollably and was in serious trouble. They were still fighting as the vehicle tumbled to the ground. It fell heavily in the field near the opium shed and broke up in to several parts. The rotor blades, still spinning as the machine fell, broke off their mounting and one blade spun towards the opium shed. It was travelling at high speed and went through the raffia screen as a knife goes through butter.

Abdullah was killed instantly as he was decapitated by the rotor blade. Hamid and the second in command rushed to him; unfortunately they could do nothing. He was laid out on a bench and a cloth covered his body.

Hamid and the second in command had a brief conversation and quickly agreed that the first priority was to hide all evidence of the helicopter. The pilot and the policeman died instantly as the machine hit the ground with considerable force. All the able-bodied men were engaged in the task of removing the helicopter. It was a gruelling task as even the parts of the machine were very heavy. It took the rest of the day, that night and all next day before all the parts were hidden; some were buried and others hidden in hastily erected sheds made of raffia.

After this exhausting work, Hamid and the second in command agreed that they would have to make a better job of hiding some of the parts. The villagers took a brief rest before they considered the burial and commemoration of Abdullah. He was buried with all honours and a day of mourning was put into practice. Hamid was very upset at the death of his cousin. He had just got to know him again, only for him to be so cruelly killed.

Since his time at his heroin estate handed down to him by his uncle Hamid had become a very calm and kind individual as proven by his treatment of the workers on the estate. All things are relative however and in real terms he was obviously still a criminal for his part in the heroin production.

He began to feel emotions now similar to those he felt when he was loading boxes at the market after the new supervisor had arrived: how he hated him. He felt hate again this time at the authorities that had caused the death of his cousin. For the time being, he had to put these thoughts aside and concentrate on the present. He would not forget who was responsible.

Hamid had another meeting with the second in command and learned that his name was Rashid. He thought it peculiar that no one ever called him by his proper name, always the second in command. He assumed that Rashid would be chosen as the head man now Abdullah was dead.

"Will you automatically be voted in as the new head?"

"No," replied Rashid, "the elders of the village will decide upon a few candidates and interview them. I shall certainly be one of the people but it is not certain that I shall be chosen or even left as second in command."

"Well I wish you luck anyway, when does all this occur?"

Rashid thought for a moment, "Probably the day after tomorrow, they will not wait long now that Abdullah has been buried."

As Rashid had predicted the day arrived and the election took place. At the end of the day the result was announced; Rashid was pronounced the new head of the village and another man was the new second in command. Hamid and Ahmed congratulated Rashid and reminded him about the arrangement for helping with the money.

"Abdullah was going to consult you as to how much you needed to tide you over," said Hamid.

"Ah yes Hamid, he did talk to me about this, we have it noted in the office." The 'office' was the store and Rashid disappeared there for a few minutes. He came out with a board and a figure of thirteen thousand Afghanis was written on it.

"Good, now we know what you want. Are you sure that this amount is enough?"

"Yes, that is what we calculated."

"OK that's fine; we will get this for you." Hamid spoke to Ahmed who produced five thousand Afghanis and gave them to Rashid. "I will get you the balance as soon as possible," said Ahmed.

Rashid was very appreciative and thanked them both again. Life went on in the village and Hamid and Ahmed talked about whether it was time to leave. They decided to stay another two days and then go home. They spoke to Rashid and said they would like a guide for the hill paths. Rashid was sad that they were going to depart but understood. There would be no difficulty about a guide.

Hamid and Ahmed were about to leave in the morning of the second day when sounds of an aircraft could be heard. Once again, the village went into all-hide mode but this time there were two helicopters circling overhead. A loud hailer startled the village with the words, "We believe there is someone there, come out and show yourself."

This put Rashid in a quandary, what should he do? The voice came again this time saying the helicopters would land unless someone answered. Rashid decided that this time the voice meant business, so he came out of his hiding place and waved to the helicopters.

The voice said, "Put your arms up if you have seen a police helicopter here before we came."

Rashid decided that as there was not a very good place for the machines to land he would be safe to deny that any other helicopter had been there. He stood still and did not raise his arms. The pilots could be seen talking to each other and a few moments later the voice addressed them again,

"Why do you hide when we come?"

Rashid shouted that he was frightened of robbers but his voice could not be heard above the engine noise. One of the pilots made a gesture to tell Rashid that he should write the answer and at the same time lowered a slim rope to enable an answer to be attached. He did this and the answer apparently satisfied the pilot who waved, and the two helicopters went away.

Rashid was glad the field was empty of fully-grown poppies as this would have been a giveaway. The whole experience told Rashid that he must dispose of the helicopter parts once and for all and called a meeting to discuss how to do this. Hamid and Ahmed left after this with a guide to take them to Ghazi rat. They were not sure when they would be able to catch a bus to Meyhabul but at least they had somewhere to stay in the lodging house.

It was two days later that the bus came and they were on the uncomfortable journey home. While on the bus, Ahmed noticed that Hamid was quiet, obviously deep in thought. Ahmed had no idea what schemes were going through Hamid's brain. If he had, he might have been much more concerned. Hamid was actually thinking of some sort of revenge on the establishment but it seemed a task beyond his capabilities. He continued to think about it.

He eventually managed to doze off for ten minutes or so and he dreamed about the village. He mumbled about fighting the helicopters and Ahmed woke him up as his apparent mumbling was really shouting.

"What are you making those noises for?" Ahmed asked him. "Sorry, I was dreaming about the village." There was a look of determination in his eyes, which Ahmed had not seen before. Ahmed smiled and said,

"Well don't make so much noise then."

He did not realise that Hamid had resolved something from his dream.

20

Hamid and Ahmed arrived in Meyhabul after a gruelling journey from Ghazi rat. It seemed worse than when they went to see Abdullah. Hamid wondered how the bus company managed to get away with such poor vehicles on a journey like this. As they trudged from the bus station with their heavy cases, he was looking forward to seeing his wife again. Hamid wondered how his wife was keeping and the thought came over him that he had left her alone for many months including the time at the heroin estate.

The two men were both very tired after the bus journey and the walk. When they finally arrived, they sat down with sighs of relief, neither wanted to repeat that marathon again, at least not yet.

Hamid's wife was out when they arrived so after a rest Hamid prepared something to eat and drink, as they were both famished. About an hour later Hamid's wife arrived; she had been shopping and was loaded with two baskets full of food and other items. Immediately after they had all greeted one another she started to tell them in an excited manner the news about a rumour she had just heard.

"Steady down woman," said Hamid, not unkindly, "Start at the beginning."

"Well I have heard that the moneylender has been arrested, I don't know exactly what for."

Hamid was mystified and said, "I don't understand, why should he be arrested?"

"All I have heard is that it is something to do with money into the bank that was stolen, I think that was it."

Ahmed looked at Hamid and said, "There goes our cheque clearing, we had better go and see him, maybe we can do something. If we don't we shall run out of Afghanis."

"Right, I agree," replied Hamid, "we had better get round to the police station." Hamid knew some of the police from his debt collecting days and he asked to see one of the sergeants. A large man in black trousers and a black pullover came out to see Hamid. "Oh thanks Abdul for seeing me, can I talk to you for a minute."

The sergeant smiled at Hamid and said, "Hallo Hamid, what can I do for you?"

"Well I have just heard that the moneylender is in the jail, is that right?"

"Yes, he is here, the news certainly gets around," said Abdul.

"I wonder if it would be possible for us to visit him. As you know I used to work for him," stated Hamid.

The sergeant thought for a moment, "We are not supposed to let any visitors in but I guess you are a bit different. You can see him for ten minutes, I am afraid that is the most time I can let you have now."

"Thanks Abdul, that's fine," answered Hamid.

They followed the sergeant into the jail and reached the cell in which the moneylender was closeted. He was sitting in this small cell about three by three metres, with a single hard bed and a chair. He looked decidedly unhappy but brightened up immediately he saw Hamid and jumped up from his seat.

"Hamid my friend, I am so glad to see you, I have been in here for nearly a week and apart from the police, only my secretary has been to see me."

Hamid explained to the moneylender that they had arrived back only a couple of hours ago from the visit to the village near Ghazi rat.

"My wife told me all she had heard and we thought we should come round immediately. What is this all about anyway?" Hamid's voice had trailed off a bit when he mentioned the visit to the village and the moneylender noticed.

"Before I tell you more Hamid, any problems for you on your visit?"

Hamid replied with some hesitation, "I will give you more details later but I lost my cousin Abdullah while I was there, but I want to know about you, that's why we are here." He continued, "We must try and help you first, what can we do?"

The moneylender looked despondent and said, "I don't think anyone can help me, I am afraid I have a big problem through my own carelessness."

At that moment the sergeant shouted out, "Two more minutes Hamid."

"What happens next then?" asked Hamid.

The moneylender thought before replying, "I have a hearing before the magistrate and then it is pretty certain I shall be found guilty. It is also pretty certain I shall go to prison for some time; possibly a long time."

Hamid looked very sad and said, "Is there nothing we can do? Is there a lawyer that can help?"

"No my friend, but there is something I can do for you. I have told my secretary to expect you and she will tell you the rest. Now go friend, there is nothing you can do. It is better that you forget all about me."

Hamid left with a heavy heart with the prospect of the moneylender spending a long time in prison. He and Ahmed talked about this at length and then agreed they had better see the secretary. They walked to the moneylender's house and as they walked, Hamid was thinking about yet another blow from the 'establishment' against him.

There was little doubt that a very deep hate against the law was building up in Hamid. He had no idea yet how he could satiate this hate but time might provide an answer.

They arrived at the house and found the door open; the secretary had seen them walking up the driveway. "Hallo Hamid I am so pleased to see you, do come through to the back room." The two men went in to the large lounge at the back of the house and sat down. The secretary said she would get some tea before they started and disappeared into the kitchen. A few minutes later, she came back and handed round the tea and some biscuits. As they drank, she told them that the moneylender had left a box for Hamid. After tea, she went upstairs and carried down a box with string round it.

She said, "I hid this in the garden while the police searched the house. The moneylender gave me strict instructions that the box must go to you Hamid." Hamid wondered why the moneylender would leave him this box but he took it and thanked the secretary for what she had done. He asked her if she knew what was really going on but she assured him she knew no more than he did. She confessed that she was very worried indeed about the whole affair and hoped fervently that it would not be as bad as she feared. Hamid asked her,

"Are you managing here, for money I mean?"

"Yes thanks Hamid, the moneylender gave me quite a lot of money when he knew the police were coming. I had to hide that as well but yes I am all right for a long time."

Hamid took the box home and he and Ahmed examined the contents. What they found amazed them; there was an immense amount of information about the moneylender's customers and his contacts, with instructions as to how Hamid could get a great deal of money from them. What was missing was any information on how they could change their dollar account money for Afghanis.

It was obvious that the contacts the moneylender had used would not be available to them. Indeed the papers made it clear they would have to set up their own chain of contacts. It did give the name of a bank in London that would help them to do this but few details were available.

One or both of them would have to go there to sort everything out. They decided that they must both go; Hamid wanted to know all that they must learn in London and Ahmed spoke English and had been before.

Hamid told his wife about the situation and they made arrangements to fly to London. Hamid's wife was not happy at all at another trip by Hamid, she would like him home for a long time.

They had just enough Afghan currency to buy the tickets with a little left over for initial expenses. They hoped they could get more to take back with them when they arrived in London.

While they were packing their suitcases Ahmed noticed that Hamid was packing the knife that he knew his father had given him. It was a curved knife, about thirty centimetres in length with a red and gold handle. Hamid had a leather cover that he kept it in.

"Why are you taking your knife Hamid?" asked Ahmed.

"I don't know really, but I have always had it with me since my father died, it was his you see. You cannot have noticed it before."

"No I cannot say I have but I understand the sentiment," said Ahmed.

After the long but uneventful journey to Kabul they checked in and two hours later were in the air on their way to London.

When they reached London, the instructions from the moneylender were to go to a private bank, which the moneylender had specified, where they should find the contact that would help them. The contact turned out to be a woman. Ahmed explained to her that the moneylender could no longer act for them and they had to get Afghanis from their dollar account, particularly when they were in Afghanistan. They could do this in London but setting up for the future was the important issue.

After giving her certain information about the account, she said she would arrange for the Afghanis to be available in three days time. She also said she would set up a new chain of contacts that they could use in Afghanistan. Hamid marvelled at the large area of contacts that the moneylender appeared to have had.

The third day at the appointed time the two men went to the bank and saw the woman. She handed them a considerable amount of Afghanis together with papers explaining the future set up for Afghanistan. She also showed them how they could access their account for sterling, which they might require while in London. After a busy day sorting out their money problems, they relaxed in their hotel room with a room service dinner and wine.

Hamid watched the television with Ahmed; it was usually the news rather than other programmes. While he did not understand what was being said, he could look at the pictures. To his utter amazement, he saw a picture on the screen of the old mansion on the heroin estate. Ahmed was nearly asleep in his chair so Hamid shouted out to him. "Ahmed, look, it is the estate!" Ahmed woke up in time to see the picture; he did not respond but was listening to the announcer. There was also a picture of an Afghan, who Hamid did not know.

Ahmed exclaimed, "That is Mohammed, he used to be a foreman at the estate before you came. He ran off one morning, he was worried about what sort of punishment your uncle was going to mete out to him."

They listened intently with Ahmed telling Hamid all about the EUDforce, and how they had caused the Afghan police and army units to attack the estate, using details from Mohammed's letter. Hamid was furious about all that Ahmed had told him; how this organisation was the cause of all the problems. He also thought that this Mohammed had a lot to answer for.

He thought of the attack on them both, the death of his cousin, Abdullah and the moneylender's predicament. He was wrong about the moneylender of course: that was nothing to do with the EUDforce. In his present mood, he blamed the authorities for everything: he wanted revenge.

He would have been even more angry had he known what had happened in the village near Ghazi rat where Rashid was now head man. It would have increased severely the feelings of revenge. After the two helicopter pilots returned from their investigation of the village, one of the pilots was not satisfied. He persuaded the Chief of their unit to let them go back and this time to drop men into the village.

The two helicopters carried six armed men each and they prepared carefully for the flight. They set off for the village with instructions to search for the previous helicopter and why the village seemed secretive. Again the village carried out their usual drill of camouflage but this time it was of little use; twelve men dropped from the sky down to the ground on ropes.

This time they carried out a systematic search and soon found the opium shed. There was plenty of evidence of the opium growing activity there – and worse, they found two parts of the previous helicopter.

Fortunately for the village, the head of the armed men was not a cruel or quick tempered man: there could have been severe retribution and death. Instant reprisals and shootings could have taken place, but the leader realised that most of the problem was fear. However, he had to punish the villagers somehow and told Rashid what he must do. "You understand that the village must be punished for not telling us about the helicopter men that perished here and the loss of the machine?"

Rashid hung his head and admitted they had been wrong but were frightened to admit the knowledge of the event. He explained that they always feared any kind of invasion.

"I know what you do here, and you realise it is against the law. I am going to destroy what is left of your crops which appear to be maize but I will not touch the food supplies in the store house." He added, "I think I am being very generous don't you?" Rashid could not help but agree and thanked the helicopters leader profusely.

The maize that was still growing in the opium field was destroyed by fire, the opium shed was destroyed and the result was a large black mess at the side of the village. Although Rashid was upset, by the sight of the field, he realised that he and the village had escaped very lightly. The helicopter men prepared to leave but the leader asked Rashid, "What did you do with the two bodies from the helicopter?"

"We buried them properly and said a few words from the Koran."

The leader looked at Rashid seriously, "Good, now we are leaving and you know we shall be watching you from now on. Grow opium again and we shall not be so lenient next time."

Many hundreds of kilometres away, in London, Hamid knew nothing of this activity. He was trying to persuade Ahmed to help him in his quest for revenge. His thoughts were about what he could do; he knew nobody in London to help. He told Ahmed that he was not going home until he could damage the EUDforce in some way. Ahmed was alarmed at this statement and tried to dissuade Hamid from embarking on such an adventure... "It is a mad scheme and you know it."

It was likely that by now Hamid understood this way of thinking. However, he was adamant and asked Ahmed if he could remember the contact in Germany with whom Omar used to correspond. His assumption was that he might get help from there, but Ahmed thought it was a vague hope. Ahmed did ring the German contact but they were not interested in Hamid's private quarrel. Hamid then decided on a direct approach; perhaps he could find someone in the 'force' to attack. With a rather anxious Ahmed providing the English knowledge and Hamid the insistent push, they tried to find out about the EUDforce HQ.

Three weeks passed before Ahmed found the London HQ of the force and Hamid was like a dog with two tails. After that it did not get any easier, he still had to find out the important people.

Sanchez carried on with his work knowing nothing of this plot against the EUDforce. Hamid continued to think about revenge, but without a clear plan yet emerging in his mind.

21

Sanchez was feeling quite satisfied after he had heard about the Mexican and Pakistan drug successes. The Mexican ship 'Rainbow' was searched thoroughly before it was due to sail and another large haul of drugs recovered. What was also gratifying was that the man who passed the drugs to the boat owner from Rusthampton, had been identified. What was even more pleasing to Sanchez was the follow up. It appeared that the Mexicans had been able to trace the drugs to a very large grower and put them out of business. Another blow against the drug barons thought Sanchez.

The Pakistan police had also done well. They had followed up on Mohammed's details of where the mule trains entered their country from Afghanistan and were able to intercept and take control of the people, again with a large quantity of drugs in their hands. Now they knew some of the buyers' routes, they could block them and clear up a lot more of the heroin; some routes would still escape detection of course, but the successes would give the police a desire to try harder. There had also been success in the search of the 'Eastern Gem': another load of drugs taken and more losses for the drug barons.

Sanchez was always thinking about the problems of his job as he walked home. He now lived in a rented house about two miles from the London HQ; a move that had pleased Rebecca as the previous hotel accommodation was not very conducive to married life. One night while walking back to his home he felt that someone was following him; whoever it was, it pretty obvious what they were doing. He dived into a deep doorway and waited for the person following him to arrive. To his surprise, it was a woman. He stepped out and challenged her,

"You appear to be following me, why are you doing that?"

The woman replied quite heatedly, "I have been finding out what you are doing to people. You are ill-treating prisoners and not allowing them to consult a lawyer. This is against all the human rights legislation."

Sanchez looked at her and said, "You are absolutely right madam, we are trying to stop illegal drug trafficking in its tracks and we are having good success. We have been told to do this by the European Commission itself."

The woman was somewhat nonplussed by Sanchez's frank admission and said, "Well I don't think it's right and I am going to speak to my Member of Parliament about it."

"You are entitled to do that of course," replied Sanchez, "and I think you will find that the British Government is well aware of all that is happening. We are all committed to break this drugs problem in any way we can. You may think we are doing something wrong but drugs ruin many, many people."

"Well I'm going to do something," the woman said as she walked away.

Sanchez walked on, not too worried about the woman, although he did understand how she felt. However, she was unlikely to have seen the problems that illegal drugs caused in the community. His conscience was clear, as he had seen the misery of drug addiction at first hand. He had spent time with the rehabilitation services in the early days of his job in the UK. He did not envy their task; it went on long after any successes he may have.

The next night the same woman was at the door of the London EUDforce station with some reinforcements. There were about twenty women, some with placards saying that human rights were being violated. One of Sanchez's senior men went out to talk to them but they took no notice and the local police were called. Sanchez did not want any problems with a crowd of women and the police moved then on, but in a very patient and quiet manner.

Unfortunately, before all was completed a television crew had arrived as if from nowhere and the pictures appeared on the television news programme that evening. Sanchez knew that after this episode, the cat was out of the bag and he would have more local problems at all the EUDforce stations. In the hotel Hamid and Ahmed had just returned from their evening meal when they saw the pictures on the television. When Hamid looked at this part of the news, he had an idea that he could take advantage of this situation.

He waited the next day near the 'force station and the women were there again, protesting loudly; once more they were persuaded by the police to disperse and they did so without any real problem.

These demonstrations went on for several days with Hamid hovering nearby, wondering how he could turn anything to his advantage. He was not sure how he could profit from all this and walked away disappointed that he could not think of a useful plan. He was still angry that the organisation had, indirectly, robbed him of his heroin estate and he was getting frustrated.

A couple of days later, Sanchez was walking home again. He could have had a car if he had wished but the journey was not a long one. He had realised for a while, that he was missing his jogging in Spain; he promised himself a regular visit to a local gymnasium to try and improve his fitness.

This particular night he was late. It was getting dark and raining very slightly. He felt sure someone was following him again; he slipped round a corner of the next building and waited. He fully expected it to be one of the women who had protested at the London force station and waited for several minutes but nobody appeared. He walked on, still with an uneasy feeling that someone was behind him, but thought he must be imagining things and relaxed as he walked nearer to his house. It was a quiet night and there were very few people about then about one hundred yards from his home, he suddenly felt sure that someone was behind him.

It could have been a slight noise like a splash but it was sufficient to make him turn quickly. He saw a well-built man, eyes staring out of a dark face and with a knife raised coming fast towards him obviously intending to kill or harm him. The slight noise that Sanchez heard had saved his life for the moment but the battle was by no means over.

Sanchez instinctively moved back to escape the initial knife attack and then swung into action to block the knife arm. He had studied the arts of self-defence and all his innate knowledge came into play but would it be enough to save him? He realised very quickly that the man he was up against was strong; he had massive arms and shoulders. The man swung the knife again and it took all Sanchez's strength to avoid being cut. In fact, a few seconds later he felt the knife mark his arm.

Realising that he might not be so lucky fighting more against this opponent, he decided to try to escape. He already felt exhaustion coming over him as he prepared to get away. Making a massive effort to avoid the knife Sanchez turned and gave his assailant a mule kick as hard as he could, which made the man fall back enough to lose his balance and sit down on the road. Sanchez then took this opportunity to run as fast as he could away from the scene. After thirty yards or so he looked back and to his satisfaction, saw that his assailant was not following him; he was picking up his knife from the ground and walking away. Sanchez noticed that the man had difficulty in standing upright as he lumbered off up the road. He called the local police on his mobile phone and reported what had happened.

Rebecca was naturally upset when he returned home and recounted the incident. She had often remonstrated with Sanchez about not using the car and driver allocated to him. She cleansed and bandaged his arm, finding that fortunately the cut was not deep, more like a heavy graze. The local police were concerned enough to report the affair immediately to the Yard where the Commissioner was informed.

Sanchez was an important person and a friend, so the Commissioner decided to put a senior man on the job of trying to discover the identity of the individual who had attacked Sanchez. He asked that Roger Taylor be seconded back to the Yard to carry out the task of finding the attacker. Taylor had carried out several high profile investigations and was well thought of in the Yard hierarchy. He regarded Sanchez as a friend as well as his boss and was pleased to lead the search. He gathered a small team of people who he knew were very good at their job and were proactive; he wanted people who also worked well together.

Taylor's first job was to interview Sanchez and to get as good a description as possible of the assailant. Unfortunately, Sanchez had not seen the face clearly, only the staring eyes, but did notice the curved knife, the broad shoulders and the slight stoop. Taylor organised all the usual things like a thorough search of the area, issuing a description, such as it was, going through CCTV and lists of likely villain's. He also had Sanchez's clothes tested to see if there was any other DNA on them. A couple of detectives were assigned to look after Sanchez when he was not in his car.

Hamid meanwhile had returned to the hotel where he and Ahmed were staying. On his arrival Ahmed noticed that Hamid was flushed and his eyes were staring: he asked Hamid if he was all right and Hamid grunted, "Yes, yes, I am all right."

He looked far from all right and Ahmed was concerned about his appearance: he looked quite different from the Hamid he used to know, there was a strange light in his eyes.

It was not until Ahmed saw the news the next morning that he suspected what Hamid had tried to do, an attack on the leader of the EUDforce. Ahmed was thinking that if Hamid succeeded in harming this man, then he might be implicated; how could he protect himself? Ahmed pondered on this all morning and found it difficult to come to any conclusion.

Taylor met with his senior detectives and discussed the attack while they waited for any results from the teams that were examining the attack area. There were also teams talking to all the people in the houses on that road.

Taylor said, "The attack might have been random but alternately it could have been planned; the EUDforce is bound to have enemies. There were some disturbances at the 'force' station so all the CCTV round there must be looked at carefully. We must also find the women who rallied outside, as they may know something".

He nodded to several members of his team and they went out to do the jobs Taylor had outlined. He allocated more of his team to the other tasks and went to see Sanchez again.

On the next day there were several developments.

Firstly, one of the women at the disturbance had come forward to give some information. She had seen the statement about the attack on the television and recognized Sanchez. She said she had noticed a man hovering near the place where they had rallied against the lack of human rights. She was not very good at describing the man but thought he might be foreign or sunburned. This piece of information, although rather thin, did encourage the search through the CCTV. It took all that day to go through the pictures but by seven that night the man was visible, briefly, a few yards away from the women who were protesting. He appeared dark as though sunburned, as the woman had said, but it was more likely that he was Asian.

The second item of interest was that the forensic team had identified other DNA on the right arm of Sanchez.

The third bit of information was from the uniformed people who had been knocking on all the doors in the vicinity of the attack. A woman who was looking out of her window had seen a dark figure near the area at about the estimated time of the attack. In itself, it was not specific but it was 'grist to the mill'.

The next day Taylor decided to have another go at collecting the women who had been at the rally. He organised an inclusion in the BBC news programme inviting the women to come forward to help. He received a good response; eight women arrived and three had seen the man identified from the CCTV. They were able to improve on the rather imperfect picture on the CCTV.

Taylor ordered the final picture to be circulated to all police stations in a wide area of the crime; to hotels and boarding houses near to the 'force' station although he realised that the latter places might not be so productive.

In addition, all airports and ferries were alerted.

It was a mammoth task and after three days with no result Taylor called the seniors of his team for a brain storming session.

22

Ahmed had spoken to Hamid about going home to Afghanistan but his friend seemed reluctant to talk about it. Ahmed was more worried about being drawn into whatever Hamid had done or might be contemplating. He thought seriously about going to the authorities but he was fond of Hamid and could not do this to him. He wanted to escape from responsibility for Hamid's actions but not to directly betray him; he continued to ponder on his problem.

Taylor had his brainstorming session but little came of it. Their quarry seemed to have disappeared despite the massive police search. Taylor ordered a second look at the information gathered so far but nothing new was revealed. He feared that the man might have gone abroad before the pictures were distributed but hoped that was not the case.

Taylor was desperate to get his man; in all his previous cases, some clue had been forthcoming but not this time. He ordered the police to go round all the hotels and boarding houses, in a radius of two miles from the crime scene and show the picture of his quarry to as many people as possible. There was debate about the need for this but Taylor insisted that it was necessary. He had a hunch that the assailant might be staying or hiding locally.

Taylor was right about Hamid still being in the vicinity but he had turned into a cunning individual and was watching the police movements carefully. Taylor also surmised that the man they were looking for might come back to the EUDforce station so several men were detailed to observe.

The next night Hamid went to the 'force' station to see if he could cause trouble; even murder if he had to resort to such measures. He wanted so much to make someone pay for all the trouble they had caused him. As he approached his objective, he saw several men not far away who seemed to be watching the place. He immediately withdrew as he suspected that these people were waiting for him to come back; he had no wish to be caught. He went well away from his objective; he would have to think of another plan.

Taylor wondered how Hamid had managed to come and go so easily with half the London police looking for him. He instructed one of his seniors to go to the station and test the system of watchers that night. The detective reported to Taylor that the men were so obvious they were useless and instructed them to watch from more secluded positions.

Something drew Hamid back the next night and it looked as though the watchers had gone. He knew he was tempting fate by going back again but could not help himself. As he came nearer, one of the detectives recognised him from the picture. Very quietly, he drew the attention of the detective nearest to him to alert the third one and they prepared to arrest Hamid. The three men rushed out together and one of the detectives tried to put handcuffs on their man. The idea was good but the man was very strong and escaped their clutches quite easily. Before the men could become organised, he ran up the road and was away. They also ran in the direction they thought Hamid had gone but saw no one.

When Taylor heard the news of the botched arrest, he was extremely angry; why three men could not hold this one man he had no idea. Like his detectives, he did not realise the strength of the assailant with his massive arms and shoulders. It was now the seventh day and Taylor still had no real clue as to the whereabouts of the man they were after, only his picture and that might not be very accurate. However, Taylor's luck was about to turn, if only in a small way.

In a further intensive search around the area where the assailant had evaded capture, a detective found a belt. The DNA from the belt was the same as that found on Sanchez's shoulder. It was not an earth-shattering piece of information but it did confirm that they were after the correct man. In addition, a hotel owner now thought he had seen the fugitive going into a nearby hotel, two nights ago. He was not absolutely sure, because it was dusk. This was hopeful but Taylor wondered why he had not said so before. However, this was not a new phenomenon... people often waited before telling the police about something they had seen.

He immediately asked the Commissioner to obtain general search warrants to enable him to search the hotels in question: this was forthcoming within the hour. Taylor had already arranged for a police cordon to be put all around the several possible hotels. He was doubtful about the strength of the hotel owner's observation but he must follow it up.

A room-by-room search of the likely hotels was carried out and the hotel registers were examined carefully. Eventually the police came to Ahmed's room and saw Ahmed which corresponded with the hotel register. The register only showed Ahmed as he had booked it in his name. Ahmed was not at all like the wanted man so no suspicion was aroused. Fortunately for Ahmed, the policeman who came did not notice the few pointers to a joint occupancy. Ahmed said nothing except the usual pleasantries and certainly nothing about his companion. No one on duty when the police came had seen Hamid so there was nothing to be suspicious about.

Ahmed now came to a decision that hurt him to carry out. He packed quickly, went to the reception, paid his bill and departed by taxi for a hotel near Heathrow. His intention was to check the flights after his arrival and then book for home. He was sad to leave Hamid to his fate but it was the right time to go and Hamid was not the Hamid that he used to know.

Hamid came back towards his hotel and was surprised to see so many police cordoning off the area. It was obvious that there was no way he could get back in to his room with so many police about; he had no idea that Ahmed had left for the airport. He slipped away to wait for a better opportunity to go to the hotel; he could see it was going to be difficult.

Taylor released the cordon after all the hotels had been checked; he was disappointed at the non-result but he still hoped for some good fortune.

Hamid saw the cordons of police being stood down and decided to have another go at getting to his room. He walked slowly towards the hotel and slipped into the lobby. He had no key but did remember the number and had learned how to say it in English; he repeated the number to the receptionist and she gave the key to him. It was extraordinarily lucky for Hamid that the receptionist who was on duty remembered Hamid coming in with Ahmed so thought nothing was wrong. If she had bothered to look at the computer, she would have noticed that Ahmed had paid his bill and gone.

It was later that she suddenly thought about the picture of the man that the police had shown to all the employees at the hotel. She came to the conclusion that it was none of her business and promptly forgot the matter. Hamid returned to his room and sat in the chair near the window. Thoughts were going round and round in his mind; Ahmed was gone, he spoke little English, the police were looking for him and he knew no one in London. He felt very weary and he sweated at the thought of the predicament he was in and started shaking. This continued until he felt completely drained of all strength and emotion. He thought about what he had tried to do and did not think it could have been him; what should he do next?

He thought hard, examining his chances. He still had some assets, his ticket home, and money, both sterling and lots of Afghanis so he was determined to get to Heathrow as soon as possible. It did not take long to pack his belongings and he crept downstairs. There was no one at the reception desk as he went quickly into the street and hailed a taxi. He showed the Heathrow name on his ticket to the driver and was soon on his way to the terminal.

He paid his fare to the driver and entered the airport departures doors, then showed his ticket to the first desk clerk he could see, also indicating that he spoke little English. The clerk took him to the correct desk for booking in for his flight but it was not yet open. As he enjoyed a hot meal and tea at a café nearby, the thought crossed his mind that life was not too bad after all. He then sat to wait for the desk to open in about one and a half hours time. Luck was definitely on his side and he did not know about the photograph that had been sent to Heathrow and all other airports. Eventually the desk opened for his flight and he booked in his case and showed his ticket and passport.

Later there was a call for all passengers flying to Afghanistan to go to the departure gate. Hamid showed his boarding card, went down the stairs and then up the steps on board. Still no one had questioned him, neither the airport officials, the passport officers nor the police. He had no idea what incredible luck he had, thanks to the inefficiency of all the officials concerned.

Taylor learned later that Heathrow was the only airport where, due to an administrative error, the pictures had not been circulated. He was not amused by this news.

Hamid settled down in his seat and looked at a newspaper where there were some pictures of footballers; he did not understand the writing but liked the pictures. An hour later, he was enjoying a free drink and thinking about his escape from the UK. He had another drink and looked forwards to seeing his wife and enjoying his life again in Meyhabul. As he drifted off to sleep, he was thinking he might buy a new car; they were not easy to find in Afghanistan.

23

At the hotel where Hamid had stayed the receptionist was talking to the manager. He said jokingly, "Perhaps that chap who the police are looking for is hiding here somewhere." He laughed as he said it. The receptionist was not amused,

"Don't say things like that, I don't like it. It makes me feel cold inside." Then she suddenly stopped and looked up at the manager with a frightened expression. She said quietly, "Oh dear, I think I have seen him but forgot all about it."

"What do you mean? Where did you see him?" asked the manager.

"In here, earlier today, I'm sure now it was him."

"Well, I had better call the police," the manager said as he picked up the phone. He explained what the girl had told him.

The policeman listened intently, then said, "Thank you Sir for that information, we'll follow it up immediately."

When the police arrived, the hotel receptionist told them that their suspect had gone from his room. As soon as Taylor was notified he cursed at another bit of late news. He organised a massive police search using an inner cordon of people to do the actual searching while an outer cordon watched for any escape. One hundred and fifty police were involved in this search. Taylor thought that if he was not found here the big question was where could he be?

Starting from the outside of a large circle they gradually moved in to the centre. One hour later Taylor concluded that he had been beaten again by this man. Why did the man want to get back to the hotel in the first place? Where had he gone?

The registers were searched again and the staff, including those off duty, re-interrogated. Taylor now knew that his quarry was gone, probably out of the area altogether. When they came to Ahmed's old room it was empty and had been cleaned. On questioning the cleaning staff it was found that a small amount of underclothing was about to be thrown away. These oddments were sent to be DNA tested. The results were as Taylor suspected; they belonged to the same man that had left the belt behind near the 'force' station. Unfortunately this knowledge did little to help catch this elusive man.

Meanwhile at the hotel near Heathrow, where Ahmed was staying, he was preparing to catch the evening flight to Afghanistan. He ordered a taxi and set off for the airport. He was halfway on his journey when a thought hit him as though he had been struck physically; it was so sudden that he actually jerked in his seat. Why should he not stay in England, in Brighton the place that he had liked, from the start of his stay there with Omar? Money was not a problem; with care, he could see out his days there. Tapping the window between him and the driver of the cab, he told him to go to Brighton instead of Heathrow.

The cab driver said nothing but nodded, he had seen worse things than a change of mind and it was a bigger fare. When Ahmed arrived in Brighton, he did not go to the Grand as he had done with Omar but chose a smaller and cheaper hotel. He determined to stay there until he found permanent accommodation. He knew that as a foreigner it might be difficult to purchase a place so he looked around to rent a property.

After five weeks of searching he was fortunate to be able to rent, on a long let, a three bed-roomed detached house in a quiet street. In fact, he was told that as long as he looked after the house as though it was his own, paid the requisite rent on time, then there was no time limit on his stay. This suited Ahmed very well and his next job was to transfer a large amount of sterling to a bank in Brighton. He hired a financial advisor to make sure his money was earning a satisfactory rate of interest. He wanted to make sure that his money would last for his lifetime.

He lived quietly in Brighton and joined a bridge club and became quite proficient at the game. He also joined a private club where he could relax and chat to others. Later he became a Governor of a local school where his accounting skills came in handy. There is little doubt that he enjoyed his life in Brighton for over thirty years and was often to be seen walking along the upper and lower promenades. He experienced one mystery in his time; he did not see any reduction in the heroin estate money except his own drawings. He pondered this on many occasions and could not understand it. Surely Hamid would want money? Eventually he ceased to wonder about it; Hamid must have done something different. After a long life Ahmed died and left all his current wealth to the school where he had been a governor.

Roger Taylor spent some five more weeks on the Hamid case but it was obvious that his quarry was long gone. There was an inquest about the pictures never having been displayed at Heathrow and someone there was quietly made redundant. The Commissioner at last called a halt to the use of the manpower and time and Taylor went back to the EUDforce but thought about his failure for a long time.

In Afghanistan another inquest was being held. It was during the time when Hamid and Ahmed were travelling to the UK. The information that Hamid had taken over the heroin estate from Omar had only just filtered down to local police and other officials like the customs people. When the Minister heard this he was not pleased; Hamid could possibly have been caught when the heroin estate had been raided. The Minister ordered another investigation into the whole matter.

The police and customs people, however, were now looking seriously for Hamid. It was easier than they thought as their man came to them via Kabul airport.

When Hamid left the plane at Kabul he felt good; he had escaped from England and had a lot of Afghanis in his luggage.

His life could now be comfortable and he still wanted that new car. As he came to the customs desks he was asked to open his luggage. The customs officer found the Afghanis and raised an eyebrow at the amount, but it was not illegal at the time. He was much more interested in the man standing before him; he looked like the wanted man, Hamid Rahim. He motioned a colleague to join him and the two of them retired some distance away and engaged in conversation. The second man looked carefully at Hamid and the two men continued talking very quietly.

At last, the first man came back to the table and said, "Please come into the room behind here. My colleague will lead the way." Hamid followed, asking what the trouble was. He did not get a satisfactory answer and a third officer joined them in the back office. Once inside the office, the customs man who had just joined them said, "My colleague has seen your name on your passport and recognised you as the Hamid

Rahim wanted in connection with the heroin estate raid the police carried out some time ago."

Hamid protested his innocence but as his picture was properly recognised and his name was Hamid Rahim on his passport there was little he could do. Within the hour, he was taken away and charged for illegal drug production and having a large amount of Afghanis. This latter charge was not really a crime but was added for good measure. If only Taylor could have seen the arrest, even though not carried out by him, he would have been very happy. The EU Foreign office informed him later about what had transpired.

Eventually Hamid was sentenced to imprisonment for fifteen years but died five years after his incarceration.

Roger Taylor was promoted, to become one of three deputies to Maurice Talbot. The general policing of the EUDforce went well and the crime rate moved steadily down.

In the village near Ghazi rat, Rashid, the head man had enough seed to replant a proportion his opium crop and for all the threats by the helicopter pilots, never saw a helicopter again for many years. He never repaid Hamid the money he owed as his letters were never answered. The village continued to exist but some of the younger men left to seek a better life in Ghazi rat; they found it hard without any skills but some made the transition successfully.

The moneylender died in prison so his secretary lived in his house until her death.

Pedro Sanchez, the man who had done so much to combat the drugs problem, retired early. He had been all over Europe getting the EUDforce stations established; the stress of this work caught up with him. He and Rebecca bought a large house on the Dorsetshire coast where they had a profitable bed and breakfast business. They found the contact with their guests good for them and they could afford help.

They lived there very happily for thirty-three years until Sanchez died. Rebecca downsized to a small cottage nearby and lived another six years.

Talbot went on to see the end of any large-scale natural drug movements in the EU. He was devoting all efforts to manmade chemicals sold to give people a 'lift' or sometimes a much more serious effect. Because of the relative ease of manufacture of these drugs from many sources, this was a most difficult task and Talbot never saw it to a successful end.

Internet crime was also high on his agenda but this too proved very difficult; the internet providers would not spend the money needed to police their businesses properly. However, in both these instances, some improvements were made and many people arrested.

Talbot retired at seventy years of age and lived to be one hundred and one years old. He lived not far from Sanchez and they met up quite often.

Franz Werner, the drug baron in Hamburg, escaped any penalty by the law for his nefarious drug dealings in the past. He had already concentrated on his casino and left the drug business behind him. Unfortunately for Werner, there were others who remembered what he had done to them or their connections.

One night, as he left the casino, he was greeted by a blast of gunfire from a Kalashnikov.

Such is life and death.

www.ingramcontent.com/pod-product-compliance
Lightning Source LLC
Chambersburg PA
CBHW072126170626
46813CB00004B/1716